Kenobi the dog is missing!

Obi felt so bad for Kenobi. He had to be absolutely terrified being out there in the darkness all by himself.

Obi remembered Boa's advice. The corn snake had
been right. If you disappear for a while, he had said,
you'll be missed. The only problem was, the wrong
pet had disappeared.

"Kenobiiii!" Rachel suddenly cried out in the darkness, scaring the daylights out of Obi. *"Kenobiiii!"*

Rachel was talking in her sleep. No, not talking—
calling. Even in her sleep, Rachel was searching for
Kenobi.

Obi realized she had to do something. She had to
go on a mission, a mission to find a lost dog.

OTHER BOOKS YOU MAY ENJOY

Gerbil ON A Mission!

M.C. DELANEY

PUFFIN BOOKS
An Imprint of Penguin Group (USA) Inc.

PUFFIN BOOKS

Published by the Penguin Group

Penguin Young Readers Group, 345 Hudson Street, New York, New York 10014, U.S.A.

Penguin Group (Canada), 90 Eglinton Avenue East, Suite 700,
Toronto, Ontario M4P 2Y3, Canada (a division of Pearson Penguin Canada Inc.)

Penguin Books Ltd, 80 Strand, London WC2R 0RL, England

Penguin Ireland, 25 St Stephen's Green, Dublin 2, Ireland
(a division of Penguin Books Ltd)

Penguin Group (Australia), 707 Collins Street, Melbourne, Victoria 3008, Australia
(a division of Pearson Australia Group Pty Ltd)

Penguin Books India Pvt Ltd, 11 Community Centre,
Panchsheel Park, New Delhi–110 017, India

Penguin Group (NZ), 67 Apollo Drive, Rosedale, Auckland 0632, New Zealand
(a division of Pearson New Zealand Ltd)

Penguin Books, Rosebank Office Park, 181 Jan Smuts Avenue,
Parktown North 2193, South Africa

Penguin China, B7 Jiaming Center, 27 East Third Ring Road North,
Chaoyang District, Beijing 100020, China

Penguin Books Ltd, Registered Offices: 80 Strand, London WC2R 0RL, England

First published in the United States of America by Dial Books for Young Readers,
a division of Penguin Young Readers Group, 2012
Published by Puffin Books, a member of Penguin Young Readers Group, 2013

1 3 5 7 9 10 8 6 4 2

THE LIBRARY OF CONGRESS HAS CATALOGED THE DIAL EDITION AS FOLLOWS:
Delaney, M. C. (Michael Clark)
Obi, gerbil on a mission!/by Michael Delaney.—1st ed.
p. cm.
Summary: When pet gerbil Obi's owner Rachel gets a new puppy, Obi is jealous,
but when the puppy runs away it is up to Obi to brave the dangers of the
outside world and bring the new pet home.
ISBN 978-0-8037-3727-3 (hardcover)
[1. Gerbils—Fiction. 2. Dogs—Fiction. 3. Pets—Fiction. 4. Animals—Fiction.
5. Lost and found possessions—Fiction. 6. Adventures and adventurers—Fiction.]
I. Title. II. Title: Gerbil on a mission!
PZ7.D37319Oag 2012
[Fic]—dc23   2011021636

Puffin Books ISBN 978-0-14-242414-8

Printed in the United States of America

For Emma,
a girl on a mission

Erp! Erp!
Girl on a mission!
Girl on a mission!

Acknowledgments

My thanks to Haley Ott, Wendy Schmalz, Lucia Monfried, Irene Vandervoort, Jason Henry, Christine Hauck, Molly Delaney, Sue Glashow and Richard Rothstein.

Many thanks, too, to everyone who read *Obi, Gerbil on the Loose!* and then adopted Obi as if she were your own pet. Without you, Obi would never have gone on a mission.

Contents

OBI,
Gerbil ON A Mission!

Sometimes things in life don't always work out the way you'd like. When your life is that of a gerbil in a cage and things don't go as you had hoped, there isn't, really, a whole lot you can do about it. Basically, you have about three options:

1. You can bury yourself in a big mound of cedar shavings and sulk;

2. You can hop on your squeaky exercise wheel and sprint furiously so that the wheel squeaks like crazy, causing everyone in the house to hear it and become as miserable as you; or

3. You can go on a mission to try and make the best of the situation.

This last option, Number 3, was the one that Obi chose—well, more or less. Maybe less than more. Okay, maybe quite a bit less. All right, all right, maybe quite a lot less!

Look, how about you just read the story and decide for yourself!

Chapter One A Real Mystery

Rachel was acting so weird. Right from the moment she had woken up, in fact, the weirdness began.

Obi had been sound asleep in her cage, which sat atop Rachel's dresser, when she heard a loud *THUMP!*

"What was *that?*" cried Obi in alarm, suddenly wide awake. She popped her head up out of the big mound of cedar shavings she was nestled under and glanced about the bedroom.

Obi stared in astonishment. Rachel had just leaped down from her bunk bed! Rachel, who was in fourth grade and slept on the top bed of a bunk bed, had bounced out of bed! Rachel was *not* a bouncer-out-of-bedder! Usually when Rachel got out of bed, she took the much quieter (and as far as Obi was concerned, far more civilized) method of climbing down the bunk bed ladder.

"Good morning, Obi!" said Rachel with a bright, cheerful smile.

Obi, blinking, glanced at the iPod alarm clock that sat on Rachel's desk. It was still silent. Usually, Rachel didn't wake up until her iPod began to play music. What was Rachel doing up when her iPod had yet to go off? Didn't she know it was summer and she had no school today? Rachel could still be sleeping! *Obi* could still be sleeping!

Then Rachel did another startling thing. Still in her pajamas, she left her bedroom, then returned a few minutes later with a pair of scissors, a dispenser of Scotch tape, a roll of wrapping paper, and a little object that Obi was unable to make out. Rachel went to the corner of her bedroom, plopped down on the floor, and, with her back to Obi, unrolled a section of the wrapping paper.

Obi could hear *snip, snip, snip* as Rachel sliced off a piece of wrapping paper with the scissors. Why was Rachel being so secretive? How could she possibly keep a secret from Obi, her  beloved gerbil? They didn't keep secrets from each other! Well, maybe Obi had a few secrets that Rachel didn't know about—for instance, Obi knew how to slip out of her cage all on her own—but, hey, *that* was different!

Dying of curiosity, Obi rose up onto her hind legs to try and see what Rachel was doing. No sooner had Obi done this, though, than Rachel glanced over her shoulder and exclaimed, "No peeking!"

Obi was shocked. How did Rachel know Obi had been trying to peek? Did she have eyes in the back of her head? Obi quickly dropped back down on all four legs.

Obi heard the sound of Scotch tape being ripped from its dispenser. Then Rachel stood and, holding one hand behind her back, came over to her dresser and Obi's cage. Obi, who was up in her bedroom tower, scampered down the tube that connected her bedroom tower to the living-room part of her cage. (Obi's living room was also her kitchen, dining room, exercise room, and front hallway.)

Using her hand that wasn't hiding anything, Rachel took Obi out of her cage and set the gerbil down on top of the dresser.

Then Rachel said, "Guess what today is, Obi?"

So *that* was it! It was some special day! *That* was why Rachel was acting so strangely! But what special day could it be? So far as Obi knew, it was just a hot, steamy morning in early July.

"IT'S YOUR BIRTHDAY, SILLY!" cried Rachel.

It *was?!* Obi had no idea! Well! This *was* a special day! A *very* special day!

"You thought I forgot your birthday, didn't you?"

If Obi only knew how to speak Human, she would have replied, "No, Mom, it's *me* who forgot!" But, alas, Obi could not speak Human; nor, for that matter, could Rachel speak Gerbil. As a result, communication between the two of them could be rather trying at times.

"Look what I got for you, you lucky gerbil!"

Rachel pulled her hand out from behind her back. She opened her fist in front of Obi's face. There, in her palm, was a little wrapped present that was about the size of a rubber eraser. Obi stared at the present, thrilled, wondering what it could possibly be. (She hoped it wasn't a rubber eraser.) Obi stepped closer to investigate. She sniffed. She could smell  Scotch tape, which wasn't surprising considering Rachel had used so much of it to wrap the present. Then, suddenly, Obi smelled something else—something delicious!

Oh, my gosh! thought Obi, sniffing excitedly. *Oh, my gosh! Oh, my gosh! It's–it's–it's—*

"It's cheddar cheese, Obi!" exclaimed Rachel as if

she could read Obi's thoughts. She ripped off the wrapping paper and placed the small chunk of cheese on the dresser in front of Obi.

Obi was so touched. Tears filled her eyes. Cheddar was Obi's favorite kind of cheese. What a wonderful mother she had! Obi had to be the luckiest gerbil in the world to be Rachel's pet. Tilting her head back, Obi gazed lovingly up at her adoptive mother's beaming face.

Just then, over in the doorway, Obi heard a voice, a man's voice, Mr. Armstrong's voice.

"Well, well, well! Look who's up! How's the birthday girl today?"

Obi, startled, peered over at the doorway and saw Mr. Armstrong enter the room, followed by Mrs. Armstrong. They both had big smiles on their faces. Mr. Armstrong had a small, handheld video camcorder; Mrs. Armstrong had a small, digital still camera.

Obi couldn't believe it. Mr. and Mrs. Armstrong had come to wish Obi a happy birthday, too! Wow, this really *was* a special day! But then Obi realized something odd. Mr. Armstrong had said "birthday girl," not "birthday boy." Mr. Armstrong was under the impression— the *mistaken* impression—that Obi was a male gerbil. So why had he said, "How's the birthday *girl* today?"

Shouldn't he have said, "How's the birthday *boy* today?"

Rachel turned to her father and mother and, smiling, said, "I'm fantastic! How could I not be? It's my birthday!"

It was *Rachel's* birthday, too? Then Obi realized that, yes, of course it was Rachel's birthday, too! After all, Obi had once been Rachel's birthday present. Mr. Armstrong and Rachel had gone to the pet store together and picked out Obi. At the time, Obi was only a few days old. (So, technically, today really wasn't Obi's birthday, but the day Rachel chose to observe it.) Nobody knew whether Obi was a male or a female gerbil. Not even Rachel. Everyone had just assumed that Obi was a male gerbil. Which was why Rachel had given Obi a boy's name. She had named Obi after her favorite character in *Star Wars*: the great Jedi knight, Obi-Wan Kenobi.

"We have something for you," said Mrs. Armstrong.

"You do?" said Rachel, all excited. "What?"

Obi couldn't wait to see what Mr. and Mrs. Armstrong had gotten Rachel for her birthday. But then, to Obi's great dismay, Rachel whisked Obi up in her hand and put the little gerbil and her piece of birthday cheese into her cage and closed the door. Obi, frantic, dashed to the front of her cage and pressed her face between the bars and peered out. She didn't want to miss any of this.

Mr. Armstrong turned to face the doorway. He called out, "Betsy! Susie!"

Out in the hallway came a burst of loud, uncontrollable giggles. A moment later, Rachel's two younger sisters, the identical twins Betsy and Susie, entered the bedroom, giggling like mad, each holding one end of a large box that was festively wrapped in colorful polka-dotted paper. On top of the box was an enormous blue bow. The girls set the present down on the floor in the middle of Rachel's bedroom.

"What's *this*?" asked Rachel, her eyes wide with excitement.

"Just open it and find out!" a boy's cranky voice snapped from the bedroom doorway. Obi shifted her gaze from the big present on the floor to the doorway. Rachel's older brother, Craig, was now in the doorway, leaning against the doorjamb. He looked like he had just woken up: he was dressed in black gym shorts, a T-shirt, and his hair was all mussed up. What was Craig doing here? Craig never came into Rachel's bedroom—well, not unless he thought Rachel had taken something of his that he wanted back.

Then Obi noticed that more company had arrived. The three cats, Sugar Smacks, Sweetie Smoochkins, and Honey Buns, had joined the party as well.

Obi stared at the present. What was in this large, mysterious present that had drawn all of the Armstrongs, plus the three cats, to Rachel's bedroom?

Rachel dropped down onto the carpeted floor to open her present. As she went to remove the big, blue bow, the present suddenly began to quake! Loud scratching sounds erupted from within the box!

Rachel let out a startled scream and sprang back. This caused the rest of her family to roar with laughter. Even that sourpuss Craig couldn't resist a chuckle. Then Rachel, too, laughed at her own frightened reaction.

But Obi wasn't laughing. There was a living, breathing, furiously scratching thing inside that box. Whatever it was, it sounded terribly desperate to get out and enter their lives.

What's in there?" Rachel asked as she eyed the present warily.

"You'll have to open it and find out," said Mr. Armstrong, smiling in amusement at how apprehensive Rachel had suddenly become about opening her birthday present.

"C'mon, just open it, will ya!" said Craig, being his usual jolly self.

Rachel tore off a piece of the wrapping paper, revealing a cardboard box. Then she ripped off another piece, a bigger piece, of the wrapping paper. More of the brown box showed. The scratching inside the box grew louder, more frantic. So did Obi's heartbeat! She had an uneasy feeling about this present. A *very* uneasy feeling!

Rachel pulled off the last piece of wrapping paper. The side of the box had the word FRAGILE printed across it, in big letters. Rachel was about to lift the box flaps when Mr. Armstrong did a very unexpected and, to Obi, annoying thing. To get a better view of Rachel's face on his video camera, Mr. Armstrong stepped in front of Rachel's dresser, blocking Obi's view of Rachel and the present.

"Hey!" cried Obi.

Just as Obi said this, she heard Rachel blurt out, "Ohhhhhhh! Wow! He's soooooo cuuuuuutttte!"

Obi frowned. *Who* was so cute? Anxious to find out, Obi got on her hind legs and stretched her neck to try and see past Mr. Armstrong. No luck. She tried jumping from side to side.

"Oh, Mom! Dad! Thank you so, so much!" gushed Rachel. "I just *love* him!"

Obi froze. *Love?!* What did Rachel just *love*? Obi peered curiously about the room. Mrs. Armstrong was smiling as she aimed her small camera at Rachel and took photo after photo. Betsy and Susie were seated on the floor, with the most enraptured, gooey-eyed looks on their faces. Even crabby, cranky Craig was grinning! What was causing this magical effect on the Armstrongs?

Then Obi realized that not *everyone* in the room was smitten by Rachel's birthday present. The three cats,

Sugar Smacks, Sweetie Smoochkins, and Honey Buns, looked positively disgusted. Indeed, they spun about and fled from the room.

"We thought you'd like a pet," said Mr. Armstrong as he filmed Rachel on his video camera. Obi stared at Mr. Armstrong—well, at the back of his big, hairy, scruffy neck. *A pet?!* Mr. and Mrs. Armstrong had gotten Rachel another pet?! What about Obi? Wasn't *she* Rachel's pet? Of course she was! Why had the Armstrongs gotten Rachel another pet? She didn't need another pet! She had *Obi!*

"This is the *best* present ever!" exclaimed Rachel.

Obi was stunned. The *best* present ever!? How could Rachel say such a thing? Hadn't Obi been the *best* present ever? Obi told herself that Rachel was just excited and not thinking clearly. Either that, or she meant this was the best present ever for *this* particular birthday. Yes, that was it! It had to be!

Obi was about to lose it, she was so fraught with anxiety and so desperate to find out who this new pet was. She *had* to get Mr. Armstrong to move so she could see. Whirling about, Obi leaped onto her exercise wheel. She began to sprint like mad. This, in turn, caused her exercise wheel to squeak like mad. Obi glanced over,

15

hoping Mr. Armstrong would hear all the squeaking and get the hint.

"C'mon, Mr. Armstrong, you big oaf, move!" Obi exclaimed, running even faster.

And then, to Obi's horror, Mr. Armstrong, still filming, turned and frowned at Obi. Oh, my gosh, he hadn't heard her call him a big oaf, had he?! Terrified, Obi stopped. Then, as if Mr. Armstrong all of a sudden understood, he stepped out of the way. As he did so, Obi got a spectacular view of Rachel seated on her bedroom floor beside the opened box and heaps of crumpled wrapping paper. Seated on either side of her, like two matching bookends, were Betsy and Susie. Obi's mouth dropped open and her eyes widened at the sight of what Rachel was holding in her lap.

It was a dog—a cute, fluffy, golden retriever puppy. The little thing was licking Rachel's hand and wagging its small tail and looking absolutely delighted to be Rachel's new pet!

Chapter Three

But . . . But . . . That's My Name!

DOG?

FLUFFY? LUCKY?

Obi was horrified at what she was seeing. Rachel was giving the puppy the Special Pet Treatment: she was hugging and petting him and nuzzling her nose into his soft, furry head—all the things a pet dreams about! It was not easy seeing your adoptive mother being so affectionate to another pet.

"What are you going to name him?" Mr. Armstrong asked.

"I don't know," replied Rachel, scratching the puppy under his chin.

Rachel never scratched Obi under *her* chin!

"I think you should name him Dog," said Craig.

Obi frowned at Craig. What kind of name was *that?* Actually, it was the kind of name you'd expect from someone who had named his pet *corn* snake "Boa." Craig had two pets: a snake named Boa and a tarantula named Jose. Neither one ever left Craig's bedroom.

"How about the name Lucky?" asked Susie—or was it Betsy? Obi could never tell which twin was which.

"I like the name Fluffy," said the other twin.

"Well, it's Rachel's puppy," said Mrs. Armstrong. "She gets to name him."

"So, Rach, what his name?" asked Mr. Armstrong again.

Rachel held the puppy up in the air and faced him toward her so that his nose and her nose practically touched.

Obi, seeing this, felt a sharp pang of envy. Rachel had never held *her* nose-to-nose like that!

"I'm going to name him . . ." Rachel paused for a moment as she tried to think of a name. Then a big smile spread across her face. "I'm going to name him Kenobi!" she declared.

Obi blinked, frowned. *Kenobi?!* But . . . but . . . but that was *Obi's* name! She had been named after the great Jedi knight, Obi-Wan Kenobi.

"I *like* that name!" said Mrs. Armstrong.

"The puppy likes it, too!" said Betsy—or was it Susie? "Look, he's so happy, he's wagging his tail!"

Obi gazed at the puppy. He was indeed wagging his

tail. Then Obi realized the puppy wasn't wagging his tail because he was happy about his new name. He was wagging it because three humans—Rachel, Betsy, and Susie—were all petting him at the same time. Hey, if three humans petted Obi all at the same time, she, too, would wag her tail.

Mrs. Armstrong leaned down and scratched one of the puppy's ears. Mrs. Armstrong had never scratched one of *Obi*'s ears! "Hey there, Kenobi!" she said.

"Well, guys," said Mr. Armstrong, moving toward the doorway, "some of us have errands to do. Anyone care to join me?" He peered at Craig, who still stood in the doorway, and said, "How about it, Craig?"

"I don't think so," replied Craig, and disappeared from the room.

Mr. Armstrong chuckled at Craig's response. Then he said, "How about it, Betsy and Susie? Want to come with Daddy?"

"I want to stay here with Kenobi!" said Betsy—or was it Susie?

"I think we should leave Rachel and Kenobi alone for a while," said Mrs. Armstrong. "They need to bond."

Obi's mouth fell open. She gaped at Mrs. Armstrong. *Bond?! BOND??!!* Rachel was already giving Kenobi the

Special Pet Treatment! How much more *bonding* did they need to do?

"I think that's an excellent idea!" said Mr. Armstrong. "C'mon, girls, I'll get you both a doughnut on our way to the grocery store."

Each girl gave the puppy one final pat on the head, and then they got up and left the room with Mr. Armstrong.

"So you like your new puppy?" Mrs. Armstrong asked Rachel.

"Oh, I *love* him!"

There it was again, the "love" word!

"Daddy and I got Kenobi for you because we know you've always wanted a puppy."

Obi stared at Mrs. Armstrong. *This* was news to her! She'd never heard Rachel say anything about wanting a puppy!

"Thank you so much for Kenobi!" said Rachel. The girl sprang to her feet and gave her mother a big, heartfelt hug.

After Mrs. Armstrong left the room, Rachel picked the puppy off the floor. "C'mon, Kenobi," she said. "There's someone I'd like you to meet."

Obi was so frazzled by all that had just happened,

it took her a moment to realize *she* was that *someone*. Rachel brought Kenobi over to the dresser and held the puppy close to Obi's cage. She held Kenobi high enough so he'd be able to see above the postcards that lined the bottom of the outside of Obi's cage. Rachel had gotten the postcards when she and her family had gone on vacation. She had brought the postcards back to decorate Obi's cage. They faced inward, toward Obi's living room, giving her pretty scenes of faraway places to look at.

"Hey, Obi, I'd like you to meet Kenobi," said Rachel.

Being the polite gerbil she was, Obi pretended to be perfectly delighted to meet the puppy.

"Hawo!" said Obi.

Kenobi let out a loud bark. Although Kenobi was a dog, he was also an animal—so Obi was able to understand him. And Kenobi was able to understand her, too. "Hey, what's this?" he asked excitedly, squirming about in Rachel's hands.

Kenobi's bark frightened Obi. The little gerbil leaped back, startled. Suddenly, as if scaring the daylights out of Obi wasn't bad enough, the puppy snatched one of Obi's postcards in his mouth! It was her favorite postcard—the one that said *Greetings from Cape Cod*.

Obi was appalled. "Mom!" she cried. "He's got my postcard!"

"Kenobi, don't eat that!" exclaimed Rachel as she quickly pulled the postcard out of the puppy's mouth. She stuck the postcard back where it had been.

Obi stared at the postcard in dismay. It had only been in Kenobi's mouth a few seconds. Yet, in that short time, Kenobi had not only mangled one scalloped corner, but he had slobbered all over the wonderful photo of the humans in their swimsuits. It was totally ruined! Obi, furious, glared at the puppy.

Obi expected Rachel to really give it to Kenobi. But to Obi's astonishment, she didn't. In fact, Rachel didn't say one harsh word to the puppy!

Not one!

Instead, Rachel placed Kenobi down on her bedroom

carpet. Then she, too, plopped down and—as unbeliev-able as this may sound, considering what Kenobi had just done—began to *play* with the puppy!

Obi, watching, groaned. She was beginning to see how things were going to be from here on out. This puppy, this Kenobi, had been in Obi's life for less than a half hour, and already Obi *hated* him.

"Okay, Kenobi, I'm going to teach you some tricks now," said Rachel. "First, I'm going to teach you how to stay. Now, when I say 'stay,' you stay right where you are, okay?"

Rachel got to her feet. She looked down at Kenobi and said, *"Staaaaay!"* She held up her left hand, palm out, and stepped back toward her bunk bed.

Apparently, Kenobi thought "stay" meant "come" because he instantly hurried over to Rachel.

"No, Kenobi, you're supposed to *stay!*" said Rachel. "Let's try it again. Stay!" she commanded. Holding up both hands this time, palms out, she stepped over to her dresser.

Just like before, though, Kenobi rushed over.

Obi rolled her eyes in disdain. If only Rachel would ask *her* to stay, *she'd* stay!

Rachel tried several more times to get Kenobi to stay, but the puppy just couldn't seem to grasp the meaning of the word. Finally, visibly frustrated, Rachel let out a big sigh and gave up on that trick.

"Let's try 'sit,'" said Rachel. "Now, when I say 'sit,' you sit, okay?" The girl pushed Kenobi's little bum-bum down on the carpeted floor so he'd know what "sit" meant.

"Now sit!" she commanded.

Kenobi bounced right back up.

Obi, watching with disgust, slapped a front paw against her forehead.

Rachel tried several more times to get Kenobi to sit, but the dog just wouldn't—or couldn't—sit. Hoping Rachel might glance over in her direction, Obi sat.

Rachel tried other dog tricks. She tried to teach Kenobi how to: (a) come to her; (b) hold out his front paw; (c) roll over; and (d) lie down. In each case, Kenobi was unable to get it through his thick puppy skull what Rachel wanted him to do.

The puppy simply seemed too wired and distracted to learn a trick. At one point, Kenobi spotted a blue elastic hair tie lying on the carpet by Rachel's dresser. To Obi's horror, the puppy grabbed the hair tie in his mouth and began chewing on it!

25

Rachel pulled the hair tie out of Kenobi's mouth. "Kenobi!" she said sternly. "Don't chew that!"

Obi was glad to see Rachel getting annoyed at Kenobi. "Well, it's about time!" she muttered.

Shaking her head in disgust, Obi took a step back and nearly tripped on something. It was the birthday present Rachel had given her—the piece of cheddar cheese. Obi had completely forgotten about the cheese.

Obi's birthday present made Obi realize something. She hadn't given Rachel anything for *her* birthday! Well, Obi would just have to fix that, wouldn't she?

But what could Obi possibly give to Rachel? As far as Obi could see, the girl seemed to have everything—including a new puppy. Obi glanced about her cage, hoping something might give her an idea. Her gaze fell upon the multicolored yogurt puffballs in her round food dish.

A yogurt puffball! *That's* what Obi could give Rachel! Yogurt puffballs were the most delightful snack! And they came in a variety of pretty colors: red, yellow,

green, pink, blue. A yogurt puffball would make a *perfect* birthday present!

Just then, Obi heard Rachel let out a loud, frustrated *"UGH!"*

Obi turned and saw Rachel standing with her hands on her hips, looking absolutely furious at Kenobi. Obi couldn't help but smile. It had taken long enough, but Rachel had finally had it with Kenobi. Feeling much better all of a sudden, Obi picked up the piece of cheddar cheese and took a bite of it. She must have been nibbling rather loudly, for Rachel glanced over in her direction. Rachel stared at Obi inside her cage for a long moment. Then, suddenly, her face brightened. Evidently, without realizing it, Obi had given the girl an idea.

"*I* know how to get you to learn a trick!" Rachel said to Kenobi. "I'll be right back. You be a good puppy, okay, Kenobi?" Then, lifting her eyes to Obi, Rachel said, "Keep an eye on him, will you, Obi?"

Obi, startled, stopped nibbling on her cheese and stared at Rachel.

Me?!

Obi felt honored that her adoptive mother thought she was responsible enough to keep an eye on Kenobi. She immediately rose to the challenge.

"I'm on it, Mom!" she cried. Obi watched as Rachel hurried out of the bedroom, closing the door behind her so Kenobi wouldn't wander out of the room.

Obi glanced about for Kenobi. The puppy had vanished.

"Kenobi?" she called out. "Where are you?"

Obi heard a growling noise from under Rachel's bunk bed.

"What are you doing?" asked Obi.

No answer. Just more growling.

"Come out where I can see you!"

Obi saw the dog's fluffy tail and bum-bum emerge from beneath the bunk bed. Then the rest of the puppy appeared. Obi gasped in horror. Kenobi had one of Rachel's pink slippers in his mouth!

"No, no, no!" exclaimed Obi. "That's *Mom's* slipper! Don't chew on that!"

But Kenobi didn't listen. He tossed the slipper across the floor and then pounced on it and then began chewing on it again.

"Do I have to come down there?" demanded Obi.

Apparently, she did! The little puppy kept right on chewing Rachel's slipper.

Obi threw her two front paws up into the air in exasperation. *"Ugh!"* she groaned—just the way Rachel had moments ago.

Then Obi did something that none of the Armstrongs, including Rachel, knew Obi could do. She rose up onto her hind legs and, with her two front paws, pushed open the little square door that was in the middle of the front of her cage. Obi was about to head out when she remembered her birthday present to Rachel. She ran over to her food dish, grabbed a blue yogurt puffball—Obi's favorite flavor—and placed it in her mouth. "Mmm, yummy!" murmured Obi as she hurried back to the front of her cage.

With the yogurt puffball in her mouth, Obi pulled herself up into the square opening and hopped out onto Rachel's dresser. She set the yogurt puffball carefully down on top of the dresser, so Rachel would be sure to discover it. Then Obi hurried across the dresser to the lamp cord that belonged to the lamp on the dresser. Obi grabbed hold of the cord with her two front paws and, like a human firefighter descending a firehouse pole, slid down to the carpet and rushed to the rescue of Rachel's pink slipper.

Obi dashed over to where Kenobi was tussling with the slipper. He was chewing on the toe. "Stop chewing Mom's slipper!" Obi ordered.

Kenobi paid no attention to her, though!

Obi gave the puppy her fiercest, most disapproving glare. "Did you hear me?" she cried.

"Don't worry, I'll save you!"

Obi frowned. "Excuse me?"

"I'll save you from this wild beast!"

"What are you talking about?"

"I won't let him eat you!"

Obi rolled her eyes. "Give me that slipper!" She grabbed the heel end of the slipper in her small front paws.

Kenobi, however, did not let go of the toe end of the slipper. In fact, he pulled. Obi pulled. It was a tug-of-war.

"Grrrr!" growled Kenobi, without letting go of the slipper. Kenobi, being quite a bit bigger in size, had a distinct advantage over Obi. But Obi was a very determined gerbil. This was her adoptive mother's slipper, after all. Plus, Rachel had put Obi in charge. Obi held on to the slipper as best she could. But Kenobi was just too big and too strong. Obi could feel the slipper slipping from her front paws, and she finally had no choice but to let go. This caught Kenobi by surprise. He tumbled backward across the room, with the slipper in his mouth.

"That was fun!" cried Kenobi. "Do it again!"

"Absolutely not!" said Obi. "In case you didn't know, this is Mom's slipper you're chewing!"

Suddenly, something across the room caught Kenobi's eye. "Hey, what's that?" he cried.

Obi turned to look. She didn't see anything, though. Just Rachel's bookcase. "What's what?"

"That!" exclaimed Kenobi. He raced past Obi to the bookcase. He began sniffing around the bottom of the bookcase.

"Those are Rachel's books!" said Obi. "Don't you dare chew any of those!"

Kenobi turned and peered at Obi. He had a very alarmed expression on his puppy face. "Oh, my gosh!"

he blurted, his eyes wide. He began to race about the bedroom in a frenzy. "Oh, my gosh! Oh, my gosh! Oh, my gosh!"

"Oh, my gosh *what*?" asked Obi as her eyes tried to follow the orbiting dog.

"Oh, my gosh! Oh, my gosh!" he cried, with a frantic look on his face. "Oh, my gosh! Oh, my gosh!"

"Will you stand still for just a moment and tell me why you keep saying oh, my gosh?" said Obi.

"I'm going to—I'm going to—I'm going to—"

"You're going to *what*?" Obi demanded.

Kenobi never finished his sentence. He didn't need to—he did what he was going to do. He raised his leg and went to the bathroom on Rachel's yellow shag carpet!

Yes, that's right, he went pee!

Obi was stunned, incredulous, horrified. For a moment, all she could do was stare at the big wet spot that Kenobi had left on the carpet. Kenobi appeared to be just as shocked as Obi at what he had done. The two of them stood there, frozen, staring at the pee stain. Then they both looked at each other.

"*Uh-oh!*" said Kenobi.

Yeah, uh-oh is right, thought Obi. This was perfect! Just perfect! Rachel was going to be just furious when she returned and saw what Kenobi had done. And to think she had put Obi in charge! She'd never put Obi in charge of anything again!

And then another thought occurred to Obi. *Yeah,* Obi said to herself, *Rachel is going to be furious.* But it wouldn't be at Obi. She would be furious at *Kenobi!* Who knows, maybe Rachel would get so mad she'd want to get rid of the darn puppy. Then it would be just Rachel and Obi again—like old times.

Yes, this *was* perfect!

Outside the bedroom, Obi heard footsteps. Quick, excited footsteps. Rachel was coming back up the stairs.

Obi knew she couldn't be seen outside her cage when Rachel returned to her bedroom. And Obi certainly didn't want to be seen anywhere near this big wet spot on the carpet. Obi spun about and scurried over to the side of Rachel's dresser. She grasped the lamp cord in her front paws and was about to pull herself up when, on the other side of the room by the doorway, she heard Rachel's horrified voice cry out:

"Kenobi! What have you done?!"

Chapter Six Mr. Durkins

Obi was not the kind of gerbil who took glee in another creature's misfortune. She really wasn't. Yet it was hard not to feel a little glee in knowing that Kenobi was about to be scolded.

Obi let go of the lamp cord. Being careful to stay out of sight, she crept over to the front corner of the dresser. She peered around the corner just in time to see Rachel rush out into the bedroom hallway.

"Mom! Mom!" the girl shouted.

"What is it?" Mrs. Armstrong's voice called up from downstairs.

"Kenobi went pee all over my floor!"

There was a moment of silence in which Obi imagined Mrs. Armstrong sighing to herself. Then Mrs. Armstrong's voice said, "I'll be up."

Mrs. Armstrong was coming upstairs? This was even

better than Obi could have hoped for! Mrs. Armstrong was going to be absolutely livid at Kenobi! After all, Rachel's mother got angry at Rachel when she left a sock or a shirt on her bedroom floor. Wait until she saw the big wet splotch Kenobi left in the middle of Rachel's carpet!

Obi's gaze fell upon Kenobi. The puppy was over by the bookcase, cowering in the corner, with a terrified look in his eyes. He knew he was in big trouble. As much as she disliked him, Obi couldn't help but feel a little sorry for the puppy. It wasn't his fault he couldn't hold it in. He was just a puppy, after all. Still, a few angry words never hurt anyone. Besides, the wet spot might cause Rachel to remember that Obi—her *other* pet—had never gone to the bathroom on her yellow shag carpet.

Mrs. Armstrong came into the bedroom carrying a roll of paper towels, a large green sponge, and a bottle of seltzer water.

"Oh, dear," Mrs. Armstrong murmured as she walked into the room.

Mrs. Armstrong dropped down onto her knees beside the wet spot. Rachel did the same. Together, the two of them cleaned up the spot.

"There, you'd never know Kenobi had had an accident," said Mrs. Armstrong, pleased, when they had finished.

Rachel gestured at Kenobi. "Ohhh, look at the poor little thing," she said to her mother.

Still cowering in the corner, Kenobi had the saddest, most pathetic look in his big, moist eyes.

"Oh, poor Kenobi!" said Mrs. Armstrong, her voice all tender.

Rachel reached over and pulled the puppy onto her lap. "It's okay, Kenobi!" she said in a soothing voice as she cradled the puppy in her arms. "Just don't go to the bathroom anymore on Mommy's carpet, okay?"

Obi was incredulous. *That* was it?! *That* was the extent of Kenobi's punishment?! No stern words, no disapproving scowl?! What was it with this puppy? How was he able to melt Rachel's and Mrs. Armstrong's hearts? So far as Obi knew, no other pet in the Armstrong household had this magical charm on humans.

"Not what you were expecting, was it, kid?" a voice behind Obi said.

Startled, Obi swung around. Mr. Durkins, the old, crippled mouse, stood a few inches away, leaning against the side of the dresser. He was eyeing the gerbil with a cold, stern look in his beady eyes.

"Oh! Hawo, Mr. Durkins!" said Obi. "I didn't know

you were there!" The problem with Mr. Durkins was, Obi *never* knew where he was! The old mouse was always slinking about in the shadows and sneaking up on you. It was very unsettling.

"Well, was it?" the old mouse demanded.

"Was it what?"

"Was it what you were expecting?"

Obi pretended she didn't know what Mr. Durkins was talking about. "I wasn't expecting anything."

"Sure, if you say so," replied Mr. Durkins, like he didn't believe Obi. Then the old mouse said, "I don't like him!"

"You don't like who?" asked Obi.

Mr. Durkins pointed at Kenobi. "Junior! But don't worry, kid. I know how to deal with him!"

There was something sinister in the way Mr. Durkins said this. It made Obi very uncomfortable. But it also made her very curious. "How do you deal with him?"

"The same way I deal with Mr. Armstrong. I'll drive him bananas." The old mouse chuckled as he fiendishly rubbed his front paws together.

"How do you intend to do that?"

"I'll let Junior see me for a split second, then, just like that, I'll vanish. I've already started on him."

Obi remembered how Kenobi thought he had seen something by the bookcase. "That was *you* by the bookcase, wasn't it?"

"Yup, that was me, all right!"

Obi decided she really didn't want to talk with Mr. Durkins any longer. He was too evil. "Well, Mr. Durkins," she said, "I should get back to my cage before Rachel notices I'm gone."

Obi took hold of the lamp cord in her front paws and began to climb.

"Hey, kid, when you need help getting rid of Junior, you know where to find me."

Obi pretended she hadn't heard the old mouse. She just kept pulling herself up the lamp cord. But as she climbed, she thought about what Mr. Durkins had said and how odd it was that he had used the word "when" instead of "if." "*If* you need help" sounded like things would work out, but "*when* you need help" sounded like they wouldn't. And what was with this "get rid of" business? What kind of gerbil did Mr. Durkins think Obi was? Obi realized she needed to set Mr. Durkins straight. She peered down to address him, but the old mouse had vanished!

Chapter Seven   A Startling Revelation

As Obi pulled herself up onto Rachel's dresser, she glanced over at Rachel and Mrs. Armstrong. The two of them were seated on the floor, with Kenobi in Rachel's lap. Mrs. Armstrong and Rachel were so focused on Kenobi and giving him such lavish attention, they didn't even notice Obi.

Crouching low, Obi crept across the top of the dresser, past Rachel's upturned hairbrush, past the yogurt puffball that she was giving to Rachel for her birthday, to her cage. The square cage door was slightly ajar, which was how Obi had left it. Standing up on her hind legs, Obi pushed open the door and then hoisted herself up into the opening. As she plopped softly down onto the cedar shavings that carpeted the floor of her cage, Obi used the end of her tail to close the cage door. It made a sharp *click!* sound. Obi spun about, terrified that Rachel and

Mrs. Armstrong had heard the noise. But they hadn't. How could they? They were too enamored with Kenobi to notice anything else. Rachel had a big smile on her face as she rubbed Kenobi's tummy. The puppy lay on his back, with his front paws curled in the air. He had a glazed look in his eyes and the goofiest grin on his face, loving every second of having his tummy rubbed.

Obi's eyes brimmed with tears. She felt a lump in her throat. It was very painful to see Kenobi getting so much love and attention.

After a while, Mrs. Armstrong got up and left the room. Then Rachel climbed to her feet and said, "Look what I got for you, Kenobi." She dug into a front pocket of her shorts and pulled out a small dog biscuit.

Kenobi, wagging his tail, jumped up onto Rachel's legs to try and snatch the dog biscuit in his mouth.

"Not so fast, you!" said Rachel, holding the little biscuit just out of the dog's reach. "You have to learn a trick first. If you do the trick correctly, you'll get a dog biscuit, okay?" Rachel went over to her bookcase and took down a yellow tennis ball that she kept on one of the upper shelves. She gave the ball a little underhand toss.

"Go get it!" she said to Kenobi as the ball bounced across the carpet.

Kenobi, barking, shot off after the ball. He grabbed it in his mouth and brought it back to Rachel.

"Good boy!" cried Rachel, pleased. "Now drop it!"

But Kenobi wouldn't drop the ball. Rachel had to yank it out of his mouth. Rachel tried several more times to teach Kenobi how to drop the ball, but without success. Finally, she gave up. Then, to Obi's shock, Rachel gave Kenobi the dog biscuit!

Obi didn't get it. How could Kenobi (a) go to the bathroom on Rachel's bedroom floor; (b) chew on her slipper; (c) be unable to do a single trick; and then (d) still be rewarded with a dog biscuit? It just didn't make any sense! If Kenobi had been a human, Obi would swear he was—

Oh, my gosh! thought Obi, horrified, as she made the startling revelation of who in the human world Kenobi was like. He was like Rachel's older brother, Craig! Craig was a big troublemaker who, so far as Obi could tell, never got into trouble with the Armstrongs. They always forgave Craig when he did bad things, just like Rachel had forgiven Kenobi after he peed on her carpet. Obi groaned to herself. Just what she needed: a puppy version of Craig!

Obi tried not to panic. She tried to stay calm. She tried to tell herself that things would get better. They just *had* to! Once the novelty of having a puppy wore off, Rachel was bound to grow weary of Kenobi and stop giving him so much love and attention.

Obi's gaze fell upon Kenobi down on the floor. She noticed he was munching on something. At first, Obi thought it was just another dog biscuit, but then she got a glimpse of the puppy's mouth—he had something blue on his tongue. It was the same shade of blue as—

Obi glanced at the dresser where she had left the blue yogurt puffball. It was gone! She must have knocked the yogurt puffball off the dresser when she was rushing to return to her cage!

"Oh, no!" cried Obi in dismay. That dunderheaded dog was eating Obi's birthday present to Rachel!

"Hey!" cried Obi, fuming. "That's Mom's birthday present you're eating, you idiot!"

Obi was seething mad. She closed her eyes and tried to calm down. "Things are going to get better," she murmured. "Things are going to get better."

Now all she had to do was believe it.

* * *

In the days that followed, things did not get better, though. Indeed, they got worse! Rachel continued to give Kenobi lots of love and attention.

She also continued to try and teach Kenobi tricks, but he was unable to learn even *one* trick. Obi was beginning to think the puppy wasn't very bright. But he wasn't all *that* dumb. Once Kenobi learned that Rachel was unable to resist his cute, sad-eyed puppy dog look, he used that face whenever the girl began to lose her patience with the dog. That look melted Rachel's heart! It worked every single time!

One morning Obi was in her cage, up in her bedroom tower. She was the only one in Rachel's bedroom— Rachel and Kenobi had gone outside to play. Peering out the bedroom window, Obi could see the two of them down on the lawn below. Rachel was trying, yet again, to teach Obi how to retrieve a tennis ball and drop it at her feet. Yet again, the dog just wasn't getting it. Obi sighed. How she missed playing with Rachel! If only there was something she could do to get the girl to do stuff with her again. There had to be something Obi could do to get Rachel to love her again. But what?

She needed advice! Sometimes the best thing to do when you don't know what to do is to ask someone else what he or she might do. Obi knew just who to ask, too: Mack. Like Kenobi, Mack was a dog. Who better to give advice on what to do about a dog than another dog?

Obi wasted no time. She darted down the tube to her living room. She made a big mound of cedar shavings so it would appear as if she was beneath the mound, sleeping, in case anyone happened to check in on her. Then she pushed open her cage door, slipped out onto the dresser, and slid down the lamp cord to the floor. She didn't head toward the bedroom doorway that went out into the upstairs hallway, though.

No, Obi headed toward Rachel's bedroom closet.

Chapter Eight Advice

There were many things about Mr. Durkins that Obi could not stand. He was cynical, opinionated, embittered, condescending, mean-spirited, plus he was filled with loathing for Obi's adoptive mother and the rest of the Armstrongs.

There was one thing, though, that Obi *did* like about the old, crippled mouse: he let her use his secret passageway whenever she wished. The secret passageway was an extensive tunnel system that ran all throughout the Armstrongs' house—behind walls, above ceilings, under floorboards. For a gerbil who wished to venture about the house incognito, the secret passageway was just the thing.

The secret passageway had many entrances and exits, including one in Rachel's bedroom. It was by the door to her bedroom closet. That was why, when Obi wanted to go downstairs to see Mack, she headed in that direction rather than toward the upstairs hallway. Obi slipped through the small hole by the baseboard and began to make her way through the secret passageway. The tunnel was dark and smelled of dust and old, dry timbers. Obi followed the passageway as it sloped downward. She arrived on the first floor and went straight to the little hole that led out into the TV room.

Obi peeked out of the hole. She was in luck: none of the Armstrongs were in the TV room. Nor were any of the three cats: Sweetie Smoochkins, Sugar Smacks, or Honey Buns. Obi spied Mack on the other side of the room. As usual, the old yellow Lab was lying on his doggy bed, sound asleep and snoring loudly.

Obi stepped out into the TV room and hurried over to Mack.

"Psst, Mack!" she whispered.

Mack didn't wake. He didn't even stir.

"Mack, it's me—Obi! Wake up!"

Mack still did not respond. Obi lifted a front paw and tapped the dog on his moist, black nose. "Psst, Mack! Wake up!"

"Erp! Erp! Wake up, Mack! Wake up!" cried a shrill

voice. It was Mr. Smithers, the parrot. Mr. Smithers lived in a cage that hung from the ceiling of the TV room. He, Mack, and the two goldfish, Betsy and Susie, who lived in a fish aquarium by the television set, all hung out in the TV room. The goldfish Betsy and Susie were the pets of the human Betsy and Susie.

Obi swung around and peered up at Mr. Smithers's cage. The parrot was perched on his trapeze bar.

"Shh, Mr. Smithers, not so loud!" whispered Obi.

"Shh, Mr. Smithers!" cried the parrot. "Not so loud! Erp! Not so loud!"

Obi had no idea what Mr. Smithers's problem was, but he definitely had one: whatever Obi said, he said— usually more than once! Obi tried to be understanding, since the bird obviously had some sort of defect, but Mr. Smithers sure could be annoying, the way he repeated everything she said.

"Be quiet, Mr. Smithers!" pleaded Obi. She was terrified the cats would hear the parrot and come into the TV room to investigate. She turned to Mack with a look of urgency. "Mack, wake up! I need your advice!"

"Erp! Erp! Mack, wake up! Mack, wake up! Need your advice! Need your advice!"

Obi was about to yell at Mr. Smithers to please, for heaven's sake, hush up when Mack's eyes opened. "What kind of advice?" he asked, in a deep, sleepy voice.

"Oh! Hawo, Mack!" exclaimed Obi. "You're awake!"

"Oh, hawo, Mack! Oh, hawo, Mack! You're awake! You're awake!"

Ignoring Mr. Smithers, Obi said, "I need to ask you about Kenobi."

Mack yawned. "What about him?"

"Well, Rachel is giving him the Special Pet Treatment and—"

Mack sat up, suddenly wide awake. "She's giving him the Special Pet Treatment? Like what kind of Special Pet Treatment?"

"Well, like they're outside right now throwing a tennis ball around."

Mack appeared stunned. "They—they are?"

"Rachel has forgotten all about me, Mack," continued Obi. "I don't know what to do! I'm hoping you can offer me advice. Since you're a dog and all, I thought you might be able to help."

"Erp! Erp! Help! Help!" cried Mr. Smithers.

Mack looked crushed, crestfallen. "They're—they're throwing a tennis ball around?"

Obi nodded and said, "Yeah. So, anyway, I need your advice, Mack. Do you have any suggestions on what I can do to get Rachel to do stuff with me again?"

"I can't believe they're throwing a tennis ball around!" wailed Mack. "Nobody ever throws a tennis ball to me! I *love* chasing tennis balls!"

"Love chasing tennis balls! Love chasing tennis balls!" echoed Mr. Smithers.

Obi was rapidly losing her patience both with Mr. Smithers *and* Mack. For goodness' sake, this was about her, not Mack! *She* was the one who was being ignored by Rachel! Still, Obi couldn't help but feel a little sorry for Mack. He was so old, he probably didn't get much in the way of the Special Pet Treatment by *any* of the Armstrongs.

"Well, well, well!" said a sly voice from behind Obi. "Look who's out of her cage!"

Obi knew this voice all too well. It belonged to the tiger cat, Sugar Smacks. The cat had just walked in from the dining room.

"Oh! Hawo, Sugar Smacks!" said Obi, turning to the cat. "How are you today?"

"Oh, hawo! Oh, hawo!" said Mr. Smithers. "Erp! Erp! How are you today? How are you today?"

"Oh, I'm just dandy," said Sugar Smacks, grinning at Obi. "How could I not be? I've just stumbled upon a little gerbil out of her cage!"

"Oh, gosh! I am out of my cage, aren't I?" exclaimed Obi, pretending that this was a big surprise to her. "I'd better get back to my cage!"

Sugar Smacks smiled at Obi and said, "Nice try!" Then she asked a rather odd question: "I'm a nice cat, aren't I, Obi?"

The gerbil shrugged. "I guess so. I mean, for a cat."

"Mrs. Armstrong thinks I'm a nice cat," said Sugar Smacks. "And do you know why?"

Obi shook her head. "No, why?"

"Because I'm nice and soft and I cuddle up on her lap and purr. Do you know why Mr. Armstrong thinks I'm a nice cat?"

Obi shook her head again.

"Because, in addition to being so cuddly, soft, and purry, I get rid of mice."

"Oh!" said Obi.

"It never ceases to amaze me, Obi, how much you look like a mouse!" continued the cat.

Obi now understood why Sugar Smacks had asked such a weird question. "That may be," said Obi, "but I'm not a mouse. I'm a gerbil."

"Yes, but a cat could always make a mistake, couldn't she?" said Sugar Smacks. "For instance, I could easily see myself mistaking you for a mouse and eating you. When I realized to my horror that it was you, well, it would be too late."

The cat's words sent a chill down Obi's spine. Obi was wondering how she was ever going to get out of this mess when, suddenly, she heard another cat's voice say:

"Is that *Obi*!?"

It was the honey-colored cat, Honey Buns. She had just walked in from the front hallway.

"Oh! Hawo, Honey Buns!" said Obi.

Then who should walk into the room just behind Honey Buns but Sweetie Smoochkins, the black-and-white cat.

"Fuzzball?!" she cried, surprised, staring at Obi.

Obi gave the cat a little wave. "Hawo, Sweetie Smooch-kins."

Obi was absolutely terrified. How could she not be? Not only was she out of her cage, but she was sur-rounded by three cats—three hostile cats who hated Obi and wanted to eat her. But Obi was a gerbil who was in desperate need of advice on what to do about Kenobi. Could one of the cats offer any good advice? Well, there was only one way to find out.

"By any chance," Obi said, "do any of you cats know what I should do about Kenobi? That puppy is driving me crazy!"

Sweetie Smoochkins made a pained face. "You, too, huh?"

"That puppy is a nightmare!" groaned Honey Buns.

"Tell me about it!" said Sugar Smacks. "Do you know what he did yesterday? He chewed up my little rubber mouse! I *loved* that little rubber mouse! It was my *favorite* toy!"

"That's nothing!" said Sweetie Smoochkins. "He chased me all around the kitchen this morning! I thought my poor heart would never calm down!"

"I'd rather be chased around the kitchen than have him eat out of my bowl," said Honey Buns.

The other two cats stared at Honey Buns in horror. Even Obi cringed at the thought of a dog eating out of her bowl. "He *ate* out of your bowl?" cried Sweetie Smoochkins, aghast.

"He did! The thought of that dog licking my bowl! *Ick!*"

Honey Buns shuddered with disgust at the thought.

Obi did not want to appear unsympathetic, but she really was desperate for advice. "So does anyone have any thoughts on what I can do about Kenobi?"

Sweetie Smoochkins glowered at Obi. "Don't interrupt, Fuzzball!" she snapped. "Can't you see we're having a serious cat discussion here?"

And with that, the three cats plopped down on the carpet and began to share their horror stories about Kenobi.

Obi had no idea that the cats felt this way about Kenobi. Well, at least she wasn't the only one who disliked the puppy. Then it dawned on Obi that this was a perfect opportunity for her to escape from the cats.

Being ever so quiet, Obi got up and took a small step backward. Then another small step. Then, quickly, she spun about and dashed across the room toward the little hole that led into the secret passageway. Obi dove headfirst into the hole. The three cats were still huddled together griping. They were so busy complaining about Kenobi, none of them had even noticed that Obi was gone!

Obi turned to head back to Rachel's bedroom. Anxious to get back to her cage, she walked quickly through the dark secret passageway. But when she got to the little hole to Rachel's bedroom, Obi changed her mind. Instead of exiting, she continued down the secret passageway to the next small hole—the one that led out into Craig's bedroom.

Chapter Nine

Craig's Bedroom

Obi always stayed clear of Craig's bedroom—and for good reason. His bedroom was a dangerous and forbidden place. It was off-limits to Obi, and to all the Armstrongs. Craig's bedroom door was nearly always shut, and the outside of his door was plastered with the most threatening and unwelcome signs imaginable:

NO TRESPASSING!
KEEP OUT!
HIGH VOLTAGE!
WARNING—DO NOT ENTER!
BEWARE OF DOG!

Despite what this last sign said, Craig didn't really have a dog. He had a dimwitted corn snake named Boa and a very excitable tarantula named Jose for pets.

The curtains on Craig's windows were drawn, which made the room quite dark. But Obi had no trouble seeing. In fact, she was sorry she could see as much as she could. Craig's bedroom was a mess. His bed was unmade, and his clothes and schoolbooks were strewn all over the floor. If Rachel were to ever to leave a mess like this, Mrs. Armstrong would have a fit!

Boa and Jose lived in separate aquariums up on Craig's desk. The two aquariums were lit with small bulbs, whose cords dangled over the side of the desk. Obi grabbed one of the cords and climbed up to the top of the desk. Craig's desk was covered with papers, books, spiral-bound pads, scissors, pencils, pens, an electric pencil sharpener, gum wrappers, a Kleenex box, crumpled tissues, an iPod, plus a laptop computer.

Obi went to the closest aquarium and peered in through the glass. It was Jose's aquarium. The tarantula's home consisted of nothing more than a big flat rock and sand! Jose was lying on the rock, sunning himself under the bulb. Obi tapped on the glass and said, "Hawo, Jose!"

Startled, the tarantula sprang high into the air. Then, on all eight of his legs, he scurried over to that part of his aquarium where Obi was.

"Señorita Obi!" he cried from the other side of the glass. "What are you doing here?"

"Ohh-bee is here?" said a melodious voice from inside the second aquarium. It was the corn snake, Boa. There was a loud *thud!* as Boa's head banged against the aquarium glass. Apparently, in his excitement to see Obi, Boa forgot there was a glass wall that separated him from Obi.

The snake wasn't hurt, though. Indeed, he started up a cheerful chant: "Bo-waa . . . Oohh-bee! Bo-waa . . . Oohh-bee! Bo-waa . . . Oohh-bee!"

"Hawo, Boa!" said Obi, and waved. His aquarium was also in need of some serious decorating. It was a bleak landscape of dirt and a small log.

"Señorita Obi, what brings you here?" asked Jose.

"I need advice," said Obi.

"Advice!" exclaimed Jose. "Well! You've come to the right tarantula! I am an expert at giving advice! Isn't that so, Boa?"

"Yes, that's so," agreed Boa.

"If you recall, Señorita Obi, I've been giving Boa lots of advice on how to be a predator and not a sap. Right now, he's in my advanced novice class."

Obi glanced over at the snake and said, "Good for you, Boa!"

Pleased, Boa grinned. "He's the best, this spider!"

"Tarantula!" Jose corrected him.

"You say tarantula," said Boa. "I say spider."

"I'm not a spider!" cried Jose, becoming annoyed. "I'm a tarantula! Ta-ran-tu-la! How many times do I have to tell you that, Boa?"

The snake shrugged. "Spider . . . tarantula . . . what's the diff?"

"There's plenty of diff, you moron!" cried Jose. "A spider can be an itsy-bitsy spider. But I'm not an itsy-bitsy spider! I'm a hairy, scary tarantula! *This* is why you'll never ever get beyond my advanced novice class!"

Then as quickly as Jose had gotten mad, he calmed down. Turning to face Obi, he gave her a serene gaze, smiled, and said, "So, anyway, Señorita Obi, how can I help you today?"

"Well, it's like this," Obi began. She proceeded to tell Jose and Boa about Kenobi and Rachel and the unhappy predicament she was in. Jose listened carefully, holding his chin in a thoughtful manner with the end of one of his furry front legs. Boa also listened attentively.

Finally, Obi said, "So, guys, what do you think I should do?"

"I know exactly what you should do!" replied the tarantula.

"Tell me!"

"You need to poison the puppy."

"*Poison* him?" cried Obi, horrified.

"*Sí,*" said Jose, nodding his head. "You need to bite him and poison him. That always does the trick."

"You want me to *poison* Kenobi?!"

The tarantula nodded. "You need him out of the way."

"But—but I can't poison him!" cried Obi.

The tarantula, in exasperation, threw two of his eight legs up into the air. "You come to me for advice and you don't take my advice!" he cried. "I can't help you!"

"I know what you can do," said Boa.

"Oh, is that so?" said Jose, and gave Obi a "this ought to be good" look.

"What should I do, Boa?" asked Obi.

"Hide!" he said.

"Hide?" said Obi, puzzled.

The snake nodded. "That's what I did once. Remember what happened, Jose? Master Craig got so worried about me."

"Hoo-boy, did he ever!" said Jose, chuckling. "He thought Boa had escaped from his bedroom and that Mrs. Armstrong would find him and have a heart attack. Master Craig turned the whole house upside down."

"And the whole time I was hiding under his bed," said the snake with a loud, goofy laugh. "You should try hiding, Obi. If you did, maybe Rachel would get all worried about you and forget about Kenobi."

"You know, Boa, that's not a bad idea!" said Obi.

"I taught him everything he knows," said Jose proudly, taking credit for Boa's idea.

Just then, the bedroom door flew open. Obi's heart stopped. She spun about and saw a boy with long, hair and wearing a T-shirt and jeans walk in. It was Craig. He came straight over to his desk. Obi quickly hid behind the laptop computer.

Obi's heart was beating furiously. The boy was only inches away—she'd never been so close to Craig in all her life. Craig began typing on the computer keyboard. Obi could hear the *tap-tap-tap* of his fingers.

Obi glanced over at Boa and Jose. They were staring at her, wide-eyed, obviously wondering what she was going to do now. It was a good question. Obi gave them a little goodbye wave. Then, quietly, keeping to the shadows, the gerbil crept across the desk. She grabbed hold of the cord to the electric pencil sharpener, slid down to the floor, and scurried across the bedroom carpet to the little hole that led into the secret passageway. If Craig's room hadn't been quite so dark, the boy, in all likelihood, would have spotted her. But Craig never saw a thing.

"Thank goodness for dark bedrooms," murmured Obi as she disappeared into the small hole.

Chapter Ten

Discovered!

As she hurried back through the secret passageway, Obi couldn't stop marveling at Boa's suggestion. It was such a simple yet clever idea.

That's what I'll do! Obi said to herself. *I'll hide!*

Obi got excited as she envisioned how it would play out. Rachel would discover Obi gone, grow sick with worry, and then realize just how much her little gerbil meant to her. Then Obi would come out of hiding. Rachel would be so delighted to see Obi again. Why, she might even give Obi a little kiss on top of her head—the way Obi had seen Rachel do to Kenobi. Things would go back to the way they used to be before that darn puppy came into the picture! Obi couldn't wait! Who would have guessed that, of all the Armstrong pets, it would be Boa who offered such good advice!

Obi got to the little hole to Rachel's bedroom and

crawled out. Unlike Craig's dark bedroom, Rachel's room was a cheerful oasis of bright sunshine that streamed in through the windows. Obi was on her way toward the dresser when, from the upstairs hallway, she heard footsteps.

Human footsteps! Then a voice—Rachel's voice!

"Stop squirming, Kenobi!"

Obi froze. Rachel was close, very close—like just-outside-Rachel's-bedroom-door close! There was no way Obi would be able to reach the dresser, climb up the lamp cord, and get back into her cage before Rachel walked into the room!

Obi couldn't be caught out of her cage! In a panic, she glanced about the room for a place to hide. Her gaze fell upon Rachel's dresser, and Obi remembered something: there was a narrow space in the back of Rachel's dresser by the wall. Obi was able to see it from her cage. She could hide there!

Heart pounding, Obi rushed over and squeezed into the narrow space.

From her hiding spot, Obi heard Rachel's footsteps as she entered the room. Then she heard Rachel say, "I'm going to put you down on the floor now, Kenobi. You be a good dog, okay?"

It was quiet for a moment. Then Obi heard the puppy's four little feet dash excitedly about the bedroom, racing this way and that. Didn't this dog *ever* calm down? Then Obi heard something that made her heart beat quicker.

The puppy was sniffing the carpet near the side of the dresser. The dog had caught Obi's scent!

"Oh, no!" groaned Obi.

Just then, out of the corner of her eye, Obi noticed the puppy's wet, black nose and two curious eyes peering in at her.

"Is that you, Obi?" asked the puppy.

"Yes, it's me!" whispered Obi. "Now go away!"

"What are you doing back there?"

"Nothing! Now go away, will you!"

Kenobi turned his head in the direction where Rachel must have been in the room. "Hey, Mom!" he cried. "Guess who's behind the dresser? Obi!"

It was a good thing that Rachel, being human, wasn't able to understand Dog any better than she could understand Gerbil.

"Guess what, Obi?" said the puppy, returning his attention to the gerbil. "Guess what Mom and I were just doing? She was throwing me a ball! I *love* chasing balls! Hey, do you have a ball? If you do, I'll chase it! Do you? Do you? If you do, throw it! I'll go get it!"

"I don't have a ball," whispered Obi. "Now go away!"

"How about a stick? Got a stick? I'll run after a stick, too!"

"Calm down, will you!" exclaimed Obi. "I don't have a stick, either!"

"Well, how about a—oh, my gosh!" Kenobi suddenly did a double take. Something over by Rachel's music stand had caught the dog's attention. His eyes widened with excitement.

"Hey, I see a ball! It's a *big* ball! I'll go get it! You can throw me this ball, Obi! Stay here! I'll go get it!"

Kenobi dashed off.

Obi sighed. A moment later, she heard something rolling in her direction. Then she heard something smash against the side of the dresser. It made Obi jump. The crash sounded hard and brittle, like something made of hard, brittle plasti—

"Hey, that's my Gerbil Mobile!" cried Obi in horror.

With his two front paws, Kenobi rolled the big, clear plastic globe in front of the narrow opening so Obi could see it. "Look, Obi, I found a ball!" cried Kenobi. "It's a big ball! You can throw me this ball! Come on, Obi, throw it! If you throw it, I'll chase it!"

"That's not a ball!" snapped Obi. "That's *my* Gerbil Mobile! Leave it alone!"

"You throw! I'll chase!"

"NO!" cried Obi, angrily shaking her head. "Didn't you hear me? That's NOT a ball!"

But Kenobi was so eager to be thrown a ball, he didn't hear a word Obi said. The dog suddenly pounced on the Gerbil Mobile. This caused the plastic globe to shoot out from under him. With a loud crash, it bashed against the wall and then bounced off, rocketing across the bedroom. Kenobi took off after it.

Obi was furious, just furious! How dare that blasted dog play with her Gerbil Mobile! The Gerbil Mobile wasn't a doggy toy—it was a serious form of gerbil transportation! Obi was so beside herself, she forgot that she was in hiding. She scurried out from behind the dresser and ran across the carpet toward Kenobi who at that moment was attacking the Gerbil Mobile as if it were a wild, dangerous creature.

"Stop it, Kenobi!" cried Obi. "Did you hear me? Stop it this instant!"

"*Obi?!*"

Obi froze. She peered up. Rachel, who had been seated at her desk in front of her computer, stood up. She stared down at Obi with the most startled and incredulous expression on her face.

"Oh! Hawo, Mom!" said Obi, which, of course, Rachel, being human, was unable to hear. All she heard were a couple of squeaks.

"What are you doing out of your cage?" Rachel asked.

Obi remembered the cute, sad-eyed puppy dog look that Kenobi always used whenever he got into trouble. So Obi gave Rachel her cute, sad-eyed little gerbil look.

But alas, Rachel's face did not soften the way it always did when she saw Kenobi's sad eyes. No—instead, an angry frown came over the girl's face. "How did you get out of your cage?" she demanded as, bending down, she

 picked Obi up off the floor. Handling Obi roughly, Rachel returned the gerbil back to her cage. "I bet *I* know how you got out of your cage!" she declared.

Oh, no! Rachel now knew that Obi knew how to escape from her cage!

Obi expected Rachel to announce this, but she didn't. Instead, she hurried out of her bedroom, shouting, "Mom! Mom! Betsy and Susie have been in my bedroom! They let Obi out of his cage!"

Obi stood there, dumbfounded at this unexpected turn of events. Down on the carpet, Kenobi looked bewildered, too.

Then Kenobi turned and made a dash for the door. "Hey, Mom, wait for me!" he cried. As he ran out of the bedroom, he glanced over his shoulder at Obi. "Don't worry, Obi!" he exclaimed. "You and I will play ball later!"

Chapter Eleven

The Last Straw!

Downstairs in the kitchen, Obi heard loud, angry voices. Rachel was accusing Betsy and Susie of taking Obi out of her cage. The twins were vehemently denying they had done such a thing.

"We didn't go in Rachel's bedroom!"

"How did Obi get out of his cage, then?" demanded Rachel.

"I don't know!"

"You took him out!"

"I did not!"

"Well, then, Susie did!"

"No, I didn't!" cried Susie's voice.

More heated accusations and denials followed, and then Mrs. Armstrong's voice said, "All right, girls, what's done is done. Betsy and Susie, I don't want you going into Rachel's bedroom, okay?"

"But we didn't go into Rachel's bedroom!"

Obi felt bad that she had gotten the twins in trouble. Now that the argument in the kitchen was over, she expected Rachel and Kenobi to return to Rachel's bedroom. But they didn't. Obi waited. And waited. What could be taking them so long? Then, to her surprise, Obi heard a strange man's voice downstairs. Curious, she strained her ears to listen.

It was definitely not Mr. Armstrong's voice. This voice was too deep, too dark, too creepy. Whoever he was, he seemed to be having a lot of trouble breathing. Obi could hear the man sucking air in and out. As Obi listened, it dawned on her whose voice it was.

It was the voice of evil Darth Vader!

Someone in the TV room was watching a *Star Wars* movie! It wasn't Rachel, was it?! Obi certainly hoped not, not without Obi! Obi's most favorite thing to do was to watch a movie on TV in the comfort of Rachel's lap. And *Star Wars* movies were Obi's all-time favorite movies.

The more Obi listened, the more anxious she became. She *had* to find out who was watching *Star Wars*. Obi stepped over to the front of her cage, rose up on her hind legs, and pushed open her cage door.

A few moments later, Obi was in the dark secret passageway, rushing downstairs. Arriving at the little hole that led into the TV room, Obi peeked out. She spotted Betsy and Susie—the humans, that is, not the goldfish. The girls were flopped on the floor in front of the TV, their eyes glued to the TV screen, an absorbed look on each of their faces. Obi's gaze shifted from Betsy and Susie to the couch.

And that was when Obi's heart nearly collapsed. There was Rachel—on the couch. And there was Kenobi—on her lap! Worse, Rachel was stroking Kenobi's head, just the way she always stroked Obi on the head when the two of them watched TV together!

Obi had never felt so stricken, so hurt, so betrayed! Tears filled her eyes. The really infuriating thing was, Kenobi wasn't even enjoying the movie! No! In fact, he wasn't even watching it! He was busy chewing on a rawhide bone. The *Star Wars* movie was completely wasted on him!

Clearly, things were out of control here! This was the last straw! Something *had* to be done about Kenobi! *Star Wars* movies were something special that Obi shared with Rachel! They were not a Kenobi thing! It was becoming increasingly and painfully clear to Obi that she needed to take action! She needed to do something about this nuisance of a dog who was destroying her life!

Obi turned and began to make her way back up the secret passageway. She didn't walk. She ran. When she got to the hole to Rachel's bedroom, Obi kept right on running. She passed that hole, then the little hole that led into Craig's bedroom, then the little hole that led into the twins' bedroom, then the little hole that led into Mr. and Mrs. Armstrong's bedroom. Obi followed the secret passageway all the way up, past the ancient mice drawings that lined the secret passageway walls near the attic, to the cluttered attic itself, where Mr. Durkins, the Darth Vader of the Armstrong house, lived.

The secret passageway brought Obi out into the darkened attic, behind a toppled-over black ski boot. Obi stood beside the ski boot and glanced about, looking for Mr. Durkins. She didn't see him anywhere amidst all the clutter.

But then she heard what sounded like someone munching. It was coming from inside the ski boot that was beside her! Obi peered into the mouth of the boot. In the smudgy gray light, she saw the back of the stoop-shouldered, elderly, small mouse. He was gnawing on a heavy woolen sock that was stuffed inside the ski boot.

"Mr. Durkins?"

The old mouse turned and peered at Obi. He had a string of yarn dangling from his mouth. "Well, it's about time, kid," he muttered.

"What are you doing?"

"What's it look like I'm doing? I'm chewing a hole in Mr. Armstrong's ski sock."

"Should you be doing that?" asked Obi. "I mean, isn't that going to make Mr. Armstrong mad?"

"I sure hope so!" said Mr. Durkins.

Obi knew Mr. Durkins did not like the Armstrongs, particularly Mr. Armstrong. Still, it always gave her a chill whenever the old mouse revealed just how much he loathed the Armstrongs.

Obi stepped aside so Mr. Durkins could emerge from the ski boot. "I've been expecting you," he said.

Startled, Obi blinked at the old mouse. "You have?"

"Should we start?"

"Start? Start what?" asked Obi.

"Start getting rid of Junior, of course!"

"Oh! Well, I don't know that I really want to get *rid* of him," said Obi. "All I really want is for Rachel to love me again."

Mr. Durkins's face hardened. "*Love!* What do *you* know about *love*? Humans can't love rodents!"

Obi was about to protest, but one look at Mr. Durkins's narrowed, beady eyes told her to keep quiet. There was no way she'd ever change his mind on this topic.

Just then, from over by the small attic window that was caked with dust, there was a scratching sound. Obi and Mr. Durkins both turned simultaneously to see what it was.

It was that crazy squirrel, the one who thought Obi was a criminal because she lived in a cage, which the squirrel was convinced was a jail. The squirrel was outside the window, spying on them.

The moment the squirrel saw that he'd been spotted, his eyes widened with fear. A second later, he had vanished from the window.

Mr. Durkins mumbled something not terribly complimentary under his breath about squirrels. Then, in a gruff voice, he said to Obi, "Come on! Follow me!" He hobbled into the entrance of the secret passageway.

"Where are we going?" asked Obi as she hurried to keep up with Mr. Durkins. For an old, crippled mouse, he certainly hobbled fast!

"To the kitchen!"

"Why are we going there?"

"Because that's where we need to go to solve your Junior problem."

"Oh! Okay!" said Obi. She had no idea what Mr. Durkins was up to, but she followed him just the same.

The secret passageway led past a series of primitive, stick-figure crayon drawings that showed mice being attacked by humans with brooms. Obi, who'd passed the  drawings on her way up to the attic, marveled, as she always did, at how well drawn they were.

"Gosh, these drawings are so amazing!" she said.

"They were made by amazing mice," replied Mr. Durkins.

"They sure were good drawers," said Obi. "You know who else is a good drawer? Rachel. You should see the drawings she brings home from school. Once she brought home a drawing of—"

Obi, who had been about to say "me," stopped what she was saying. She also stopped walking. That was because Mr. Durkins had stopped. He stared at her with a pinched, annoyed look on his old face. Clearly, the mouse did not care to hear about Rachel's drawing ability.

"Never mind," said Obi.

Mr. Durkins continued walking and continued with his story. "When the Armstrongs moved into this house, everything changed. It wasn't long before Mr. Armstrong put out mousetraps. When they didn't work, the Armstrongs got those three cats. Then one day my family mysteriously disappeared. Just like that, they vanished. I was up in the attic and didn't see what happened, but it must've been a horrible, bloody massacre. But don't worry, kid," said Mr. Durkins. "I'm getting my revenge! I'm getting even with those Armstrongs! All six of them! I've got something *big* planned! Really *big!*"

Obi didn't want to hear what Mr. Durkins had planned. As far as she was concerned, the less she knew about Mr. Durkins's sinister plans, the better.

Mr. Durkins stopped in front of a small hole that had bright sunshine peeping through it.

"Here we are," he announced.

Obi stepped beside Mr. Durkins and peeked out of the little hole. She had a great view of the sun-drenched kitchen. Nobody was there, not even the cats.

"Everyone is in the TV room," said Mr. Durkins. "They're all watching that movie. Even the cats."

Obi was shocked. They hadn't stopped at the hole to the TV room. How did Mr. Durkins know all this? She pulled her head out from the hole and stared at the old mouse. "How do you know all this?" she asked.

"I know everything that happens in this house," said Mr. Durkins. "Nothing escapes me!"

It really creeped Obi out that Mr. Durkins always seemed to know everything that was going on in the Armstrongs' house, at any time.

"So what's the plan?" Obi asked.

"See that screen door?" said Mr. Durkins. He pointed to the blue screen door that led out to the backyard.

"What about it?"

"Well, it's broken."

"How do you know *that?*"

"Because I broke it."

"You did? Why?"

"To annoy Mr. Armstrong."

Obi should have guessed as much. "How did you break it?"

"Look, kid, you're on a need-to-know basis, okay?"

"Okay, okay!" replied Obi.

"So here's what we're going to do," said Mr. Durkins. "You're going to—"

"Did you do something to the hinges?"

The old mouse didn't answer. He just looked annoyed.

"Sorry," said Obi. "You were saying?"

"You're going to lead Jun—"

"But *did* you do something to the hinges?" Obi couldn't help asking.

The old mouse let out an exasperated sigh. "I used my teeth to make it so that the latch won't catch."

"So what does that mean?" asked Obi.

"It means the screen door won't stay shut," explained Mr. Durkins. "It means it'll open with just a little push."

"How long has it been broken?"

"Weeks," replied Mr. Durkins. "Mrs. Armstrong keeps asking Mr. Armstrong to fix it. He keeps saying he will, but he hasn't, the lazy bum!"

"So what are we going to do?" asked Obi.

"*You're* going to bring Junior to the screen door."

"How am I going to do *that?*"

"You're going to tell Junior you're going to throw him a ball."

"How did you know Junior—I mean, Kenobi—likes chasing balls?"

"I told you," said Mr. Durkins, "I know *everything* that happens in this house."

"So what happens when I bring him to the screen door?"

"You'll tell him you forgot the ball," replied Mr. Durkins. "You'll tell him to go outside and wait for you. You'll tell him that you'll be out in just a minute."

"Then what?" asked Obi. "I don't have to go outdoors, do I? Because to be perfectly honest with you, Mr. Durkins, I'm not too keen about going out of the house. I mean, I'm fine about being out of my cage *in* the house, but outside the house is an entirely different story. I'm really an indoors pet, not an out—"

Obi saw how irritated Mr. Durkins looked and abruptly shut up.

"You'll stay indoors," said Mr. Durkins. "Only Junior will go outdoors."

"Oh, okay!" said Obi.

"When Rachel finds he's outside the house, she'll be just furious with him," said Mr. Durkins.

"She *will* be just furious with him," said Obi. "You should've seen how mad she got when she found *me* out of my cage. She thought the twins had let me out."

"Now, if you hurry," said Mr. Durkins, "you'll find that Junior has just lost interest in hanging out in the TV room. He's out in the front hallway this very moment, chewing on his bone."

"How do you know this?" asked Obi, amazed. What did

Mr. Durkins have? Surveillance cameras all throughout the house?

The old mouse gave Obi a how-do-you-think-I-know-this? look.

"Sorry, I forgot," said Obi. "You know everything that happens in this house."

"So? What are you waiting for, kid? Get moving!"

"Oh, yeah, right!" said Obi. She slipped out through the little hole and into the kitchen and raced out into the front hallway. Sure enough, there was Kenobi, chewing on his rawhide bone.

Kenobi appeared surprised to see Obi. "Obi? What are you doing here?"

"I'm here to throw you a ball," replied Obi.

Kenobi's face lit up with excitement. "You are?" he cried. "Throw me a ball! Throw me a ball!"

"Let's do it outside," said Obi.

"Yeah! Let's do it outside!" cried Kenobi.

"We can get out of the house through the screen door in the kitchen," said Obi. As she turned to go into the kitchen, Kenobi barreled past her, knocking her over.

When Obi entered the kitchen, Kenobi was already at the blue screen door, waiting to go outside. "Hurry up, Obi!"

"Oh, wait!" exclaimed Obi. She stopped as if she had suddenly remembered something. "Gosh darn it all! I forgot the ball! Look, Kenobi, you go outside and wait for me. I'll be out in just a second with the ball. Okay?"

"Okay!" He went to leave, then realized that the screen door was closed. "Wait! How do I get out?"

"Just push the screen door."

"Yeah? Really? That's all I have to do? Who knew?"

And with that, Kenobi pushed the screen door open with his front paw and dashed outside. The screen door slapped closed behind him.

Obi didn't know why, exactly, but she did not have a good feeling about what she had just done. She was about to turn to go back into the secret passageway when, behind her, she heard a voice say:

"Nice!"

Obi let out a frightened gasp and swung around. Sweetie Smoochkins, the black-and-white cat, stood a mere few inches away, peering at Obi with big, gleaming eyes and a perfectly delighted grin on her face.

Chapter Thirteen Immunity

Fuzzball," **said the cat.** "You are my hero!"

Obi stared at Sweetie Smoochkins. She was shocked. She was sure she had misheard the cat. Or was this a joke? "Is this a joke?" asked Obi.

"No joke," said Sweetie Smoochkins, smiling. "You, my dear Fuzzball, have done all of us cats a huge favor."

"I have?"

"You have! You've ditched that drippy puppy. On behalf of myself, Sugar Smacks, and Honey Buns, thank you, Fuzzball!"

"Oh! Well, you're welcome!"

The smile faded from Sweetie Smoochkins's face. The cat frowned and let out a deep, troubled sigh.

"This is a difficult situation, though, isn't it?"

"How do you mean?"

"Well, here you are, a totally unprotected gerbil, and

here am I, a hungry cat with strong, carnivorous cravings that a cat gets whenever she spies a small, desirable prey."

"Oh. I see what you mean," said Obi. She noticed that the cat's tail was doing that awful swirling and swishing thing it always did whenever she eyed Obi in a craving sort of way.

"What do you think we should do about it?" asked Sweetie Smoochkins.

"I'm not really sure," confessed Obi.

"Well, I'll tell you what I'm going to do," said the cat. "Although it goes against my better judgment and it certainly goes against my cat instincts, I'm going to grant you immunity."

"Immunity?" said Obi, frowning. "What's *that*?" It wasn't a word she was familiar with.

The cat looked incredulous. "Where have *you* been, Fuzzball? Don't you watch any reality TV shows?"

"No," replied Obi. Which was the truth. She'd seen plenty of movies with Rachel, but no reality TV shows. Obi did not even know what a reality TV show was.

"Obi, Obi, Obi!" sighed the cat. "You need to get out more often!"

"So what's this immunity thing?" asked Obi.

"It means you've done a magnificent thing that keeps you from being kicked off the TV show."

"Oh! But we're not on a TV show."

"That's true, we're not," agreed the cat. "So in this case, I guess it means you can't be harmed. In other words, I can't touch you, Fuzzball. I'm giving you immunity from being eaten up by me."

"Oh! Well! That's very nice of you!" said Obi.

"Yes, it is," agreed Sweetie Smoochkins.

"I like having immunity," said Obi. "How long does it last?"

"Until the next show—or, in your case, until the next time I see you."

Obi was sorry to hear it didn't last longer. "Well, thank you for giving me immunity."

"Thank *you* for taking care of Kenobi."

"Well, I guess I should be going," said Obi. She waved goodbye to the cat and then started across the kitchen floor toward the little hole that led into the secret passageway.

"Where you going, Fuzzball?"

Obi stopped and peered at the cat. Sweetie Smoochkins was staring at the gerbil with a puzzled frown. It was then that Obi realized that she was heading toward the secret passageway. None of the cats knew about the secret passageway. Thank goodness Sweetie Smoochkins had said something—otherwise Obi would have given away the secret passageway.

"The front hallway is that way," said Sweetie Smoochkins, gesturing toward the doorway to the front hallway.

"Oh! Why, yes! Of course it is!" exclaimed Obi. "Silly me! See that? I'm just so happy to have immunity, I wasn't thinking!"

Obi quickly trotted past the cat and went out into the front hallway. After making sure Sweetie Smoochkins was no longer watching her, Obi slipped beneath the grandfather clock and into the little hole that led into the secret passageway. Less than a minute later, Obi was back in her cage, with her cage door closed.

The first thing Obi did when she was back in her cage was to look out Rachel's bedroom window to see if she could see Kenobi out on the lawn. She was hoping to see the little puppy sitting on the grass, patiently waiting for Obi to come out of the house with a ball. But he wasn't. Obi felt a queasy sensation in her stomach. She was feeling worse and worse about what she had done.

As Obi looked for Kenobi, she spotted that daffy

squirrel who had a nest in the upper branches of the Norway maple in the Armstrongs' lawn. The squirrel was in the maple tree, leaping from branch to branch, doing his amazing acrobat act.

Obi heard Rachel's voice call out from downstairs:

"Kenobi? Where are you, Kenobi? Come out, come out wherever you are!"

Her voice sounded unconcerned, like a girl curious to find out where her dog had disappeared to. Obi heard Rachel's footsteps coming up the stairs. She entered the bedroom, stopped, and glanced about the room.

"You in here, Kenobi?" asked Rachel. Her eyes fell upon Obi in her bedroom tower. "Hey, Obe, you haven't seen Kenobi, have you?"

Obe! Rachel had called Obi *Obe!* That was the affectionate, loving nickname Rachel called Obi. If only Rachel knew the evil thing that Obi had done to Kenobi, she wouldn't be calling her Obe.

Rachel left the bedroom and went back downstairs. "Hey, Mom, have you seen Kenobi?" Obi heard Rachel ask her mother.

"He's not up in your bedroom?" Mrs. Armstrong's voice replied.

"No. I can't find him anywhere." For the first time, Obi thought she detected a trace of worry in Rachel's voice.

"He's got to be somewhere," said Mrs. Armstrong. "Unless . . . oh, no!"

"What?"

"The screen door is open!"

"Kenobi went outside?!" shrieked Rachel in alarm. "He's only a puppy. He'll run off!" There was no mistaking the alarm in Rachel's voice now.

Obi heard the screen door in the kitchen bang shut. She spun around and peered out Rachel's bedroom window. Down on the lawn below, she saw Rachel and her mother hurry out of the house.

"Kenobiiii! Kenobiiii!" Rachel called out.

"Kenobiiii! Come, Kenobiiii!" shouted Mrs. Armstrong.

But Kenobi did not come. Rachel and her mother disappeared from Obi's view as they circled around the house. Obi could still hear them, though, yelling, "Kenobi! Come, Kenobi!"

From inside the house, the twins, Betsy and Susie, must have heard Rachel and Mrs. Armstrong yelling for

Kenobi, for they, too, came outside to help look for the dog. To Obi's amazement, even Craig came out to look.

They were all still looking for Kenobi when Mr. Armstrong came home from work. The moment he pulled his human mobile into the driveway, Rachel, in tears, hurried over to her father. Obi watched as he stepped out of the human mobile and Rachel told him the bad news. Mr. Armstrong started looking for the dog. He didn't even change out of his work clothes. He and Rachel got into the human mobile and began driving around the neighborhood to look for Kenobi. A half hour later, the human mobile returned to the Armstrongs' driveway. From the upstairs bedroom window, Obi watched as Mr. Armstrong and Rachel stepped out of the vehicle. They both looked very discouraged. It wasn't hard to figure out why: Kenobi was not with them.

Obi felt horrible. She felt so guilty. Where was Kenobi? She had specifically told the dog to wait for her to come out of the house. So where was he? Why hadn't he waited like she told him to? Couldn't that dimwit dog do *anything* right? Obi was also mad at Mr. Durkins for telling Obi about the broken screen door. What was Obi thinking? She *never* should have listened to that disgruntled old mouse. Obi was also angry at Mr. Armstrong. If he had only fixed the stupid screen door like Mrs. Armstrong kept asking him to, Obi would not have been able to let Kenobi out of the house. Obi was even mad at Rachel. If she had only shown Obi a little more love and attention, none of this would ever have happened!

Obi sighed. Deep down, she knew who was really to blame: Obi herself.

That night Rachel was in tears about Kenobi—which made Obi feel miserable. Rachel climbed up the ladder of her bunk bed and flung herself on her bed and cried and cried. The girl wouldn't even come down to eat dinner. How could she eat, when she was so worried about Kenobi being outside alone at night? Several times that evening, Mr. and Mrs. Armstrong each came into the bedroom to try and comfort Rachel, but to no avail.

During the night, Rachel tossed and turned wildly in her bed. Unable to sleep, Obi sat in her bedroom tower, gazing at Rachel in her bunk bed. She felt horribly guilty. Every few minutes, Obi would peer out Rachel's bedroom window, hoping she might spot Kenobi. The Armstrongs had left the outdoor floodlight on in case Kenobi should return in the middle of the night. The

floodlight, which was on the side of the house, shone upon the Armstrongs' driveway and lawn. Where the floodlight didn't shine, it was dark and creepy. Obi felt so bad for Kenobi. He had to be absolutely terrified being out there in the darkness all by himself.

Obi remembered Boa's advice. The corn snake had been right. If you disappear for a while, he had said, you'll be missed. The only problem was, the wrong pet had disappeared!

"Kenobiiii!" Rachel suddenly cried out in the darkness, scaring the daylights out of Obi. *"Kenobiiii!"*

Rachel was talking in her sleep. No, not talking—calling. Even in her sleep, Rachel was searching for Kenobi.

Obi realized she had to do something. She had to go on a mission, a mission to find a lost dog.

Obi decided **to wait until morning** to go on her mission. It would be daylight then and she'd be able to see where she was going—which was kind of important, since she had no idea where she was going. And so very early the next morning, in the gray light of dawn, before Rachel had woken up, Obi snuck out of her cage.

The little gerbil slipped into the secret passageway and followed it downstairs, stopping at the small hole that led out into the kitchen. To her surprise, she smelled coffee brewing. Someone was in the kitchen! Obi peeked out of the small hole and saw Mr. Armstrong! He was squatting over by the screen door. He was dressed in his Saturday work clothes—old T-shirt, jeans, beat-up sneakers—and he had a screwdriver in his hand. A hammer and some other tools lay on the tiled floor.

What was Mr. Armstrong doing up so early?

Oh, no! He wasn't! He was! He was fixing the screen door! Why was he fixing it *now* of all times? Couldn't he have waited until Obi had escaped from the house? Obi had planned to slip out of the house by the broken screen door. Now how was she supposed to escape?

Obi was so anxious to find Kenobi, it never occurred to her that, even if Mr. Armstrong hadn't been in the kitchen, she could not have escaped by the screen door— not at that early hour, at any rate. To do that she would also have had to get past the other kitchen door, the inside wooden door. That door would have been closed for the night, not to mention, locked.

Stepping back from the little hole, Obi bumped into something. Something small and furry. Startled, Obi gasped. She spun about, her heart racing.

It was Mr. Durkins!

"Mr. Durkins!" she cried. "How long have you been here?"

Mr. Durkins had a fierce look in his eyes. "What are you doing?" he demanded.

"I need to get out of the house," replied Obi.

"Why do you want to get out of the house?"

"I need to find Kenobi."

"*What?!* Why?"

"I need to find Kenobi and bring him back home."

Mr. Durkins crossed his arms. "No!" he said. "That's not part of the plan!"

"Plan? What plan?" asked Obi, frowning.

But Mr. Durkins didn't answer Obi's question. He just said, "You're out of luck, kid! There's no way out of the house except out that screen door! And as you can see, Mr. Armstrong has finally decided to fix it!"

Something in the way Mr. Durkins said this, though, made Obi suspicious. "There's got to be another way out!"

"Well, there isn't!"

Obi just couldn't believe this. She was almost sure Mr. Durkins was lying to her. Obi did something then that was so unlike her, it startled her. But it startled Mr. Durkins even more. With her two front paws, Obi shoved Mr. Durkins up against the wall of the secret passageway.

"Hey, kid, what are you doing?!" cried Mr. Durkins in alarm.

"There's another way out of this house and you know where it is!" said Obi. "Now show it to me!"

"But it's not part of the plan!" protested Mr. Durkins.

"I don't care about your plan," she said. "Show me how to get out of this house!"

"No!" said Mr. Durkins.

Obi pushed the old mouse harder up against the wall. "Show me how to get out of this house, Mr. Durkins!"

"All right! All right!" Mr. Durkins cried. "I'll show you the way!"

Obi let go of the old mouse. "I'm sorry I had to do that, Mr. Durkins," she said. "But it's important I find Kenobi."

"I don't understand you, kid!" grumbled Mr. Durkins as, leading the way, he began hobbling down the tunnel. "I just don't understand you! That lousy dog is gone! He's history! You and Rachel are together again! And Mr. Armstrong got what was coming to him!"

Hearing this, Obi frowned. Then, all at once, it all came into focus for her. "*This* was your big plan, wasn't it?"

"What are you talking about?"

"You know what I'm talking about! You told me you were planning something big! This was it, wasn't it? This was how you were going to get back at Mr. Armstrong and the rest of the Armstrongs! You were going to get rid of Kenobi! And *I* helped you do it! I fell for it!"

Mr. Durkins stopped in front of a part of the tun-

nel that was covered with cobwebs. As Obi watched in amazement, Mr. Durkins wiped away the cobwebs, then slid open a secret panel. Obi had no idea a secret panel was there! Mr. Durkins started down this new section of the tunnel. Obi followed.

"I *don't* know what you're talking about," said Mr. Durkins.

"You told me you broke the screen door," replied Obi.

"Yeah, so?"

"So," said Obi. "You knew if Kenobi escaped from the house through the screen door, Mr. Armstrong would feel absolutely terrible about it because he should've fixed the screen door weeks ago. You told me Mrs. Armstrong kept telling him to fix it but he didn't! You knew he'd blame himself!"

"You're assuming that I knew that Junior would run away when he got outside."

"Am I?" said Obi. "I don't think so! I think you knew Kenobi would run away the first chance he got!"

"Now how would I know a thing like that?"

"Because you see everything that happens in this

house, remember, Mr. Durkins? You've seen Kenobi. You know he's got squish-squish for a brain and as soon as he got outside, he'd run off and get lost."

"Look, kid—"

"And another thing, Mr. Durkins! Stop calling me *kid*! My name is *Obi*!"

Mr. Durkins stopped and turned to face Obi. He held out his paw toward a small hole in the wall of the secret passageway. Bright sunlight was peeping through the hole.

"Well, Obi," he said. "Here we are! Here's the way to get out of the house."

Obi stepped in front of the little opening and peered out. She saw a big green, leafy bush and, beyond that, a green lawn. She had no idea if she was looking out at the front yard or the backyard or a side of the house.

"Well, what are you waiting for, *Obi*?" asked Mr. Durkins. "You're not scared to go outside, are you?"

Actually, she was. She was petrified. It was one thing to tell yourself that you were going to go on a mission outside the house; it was another thing to actually go and do it. Who knew what dangers lurked outside the house for a little gerbil?

Obi could feel Mr. Durkins eyeing her closely. She did not want him to see that she was having second thoughts about venturing outside the house.

"Well, thank you, Mr. Durkins, for showing me the way," she said.

Then Obi took a deep breath, closed her eyes, and leaped out of the hole.

Chapter Fifteen

A Strange, Rustling Sound

Obi could feel her heart hammering inside her chest as, eyes closed, she fell through the air. With a *ploff!*, she landed on something hard yet soft and gushy. She opened her eyes and saw she had landed on—

Obi shrieked!

The thing she landed on shrieked!

It was—it was a big brown toad! It had warts all over its body! Big ugly warts! Obi had never seen a toad—well, not a real-life-flesh-and-blood-and-covered-with-warts one. She'd only seen pictures of toads in the books Mr. Armstrong read to Rachel.

"Hey, watch it, will ya!" exclaimed the big toad indignantly and hopped off in a huff.

"Sorry!" Obi called out after him.

Obi hadn't been outdoors for more than a few seconds and already she'd nearly killed a toad! Obi told herself she really needed to be more careful. Clearly, being out-doors was a lot more dangerous than being indoors. Plus, if she got into trouble, there would be no Rachel to come to her rescue.

Obi wanted to start out on her mission to find Kenobi. The only problem was, she hadn't the slightest clue where to go. Obi turned back to the house. It took her a moment before she spotted the small opening to the secret passageway. It was behind a coiled green garden hose that hung from the clapboard, just above the cement foundation. Obi made a mental note of the little hole so she'd be able to find it later. Lifting her eyes higher, Obi spotted Rachel's upstairs bedroom window—the one Obi looked out from when she was in her cage.

"Well, for heaven's sake!" exclaimed Obi, realizing where she was now. "I'm in the Armstrongs' backyard!"

Happy to know this, Obi started on her way. She padded under a bush and across a soft bed of black mulch until she arrived at the Armstrongs' back lawn. Obi had never walked on grass before. To be honest, she wasn't entirely sure she liked it. For one thing, the grass needed mowing; the grass was so tall, it made it difficult to see very far ahead. How was she supposed to find Kenobi?

Obi started to make her way across the lawn. She hadn't gone very far when she heard something in the grass behind her. It was a strange, rustling sound.

Obi, terrified, stopped. The moment she did, the sound stopped. Obi nervously glanced over her shoulder. All she saw was tall, jagged green grass.

"Hawo?" Obi called out. "Who's there?"

There was no answer.

Feeling very vulnerable, Obi started walking again. The strange, rustling sound started up again.

Obi froze in her tracks. The rustling sound instantly ceased. Obi spun about. Once again, all she saw was lots of tall, unmowed grass.

"Hawo? Anyone there?"

Still no answer.

By now, Obi's heart was thumping furiously. She walked faster. To Obi's horror, the strange, rustling sound began moving faster. What was following her? Was it one of the cats? It wasn't a hungry fox, was it? Or a starving coyote? Or maybe it was a—

Stop it! Obi told herself. *Just stop it! You're freaking yourself out!*

As Obi continued on her way, she repeatedly glanced over her shoulder, hoping to see who was following her. Why did the darn grass have to be so gosh darn high? Didn't Mr. Armstrong *ever* mow this lawn? Apparently, fixing a screen door wasn't the only thing he put off doing!

It was then that Obi remembered the woodpile that was at the edge of the Armstrongs' backyard, by the woods. Obi saw it every day from her cage when she gazed out of Rachel's bedroom window. If Obi could get to the woodpile, she could hide in between one of the logs.

Obi abruptly stopped. Just as she had hoped, the strange, rustling sound also stopped. Obi waited a moment, and then, hoping to catch whatever it was that was following her off-guard, she took off like a missile.

Obi ran as fast as she could. Because she ran every day on her exercise wheel, Obi was in fantastic shape. There was no way the creature would be able to keep up with *this* speedy gerbil!

Yet, incredulously, the thing *did* keep up! Not only that, but Obi heard the creature closing in on her! Obi shrieked and ran even faster through the tall grass. When she got to the end of the lawn, Obi took a flying leap into the air toward the woodpile. She landed on top of a birch log that had white, peeling bark. Obi quickly sprang to her feet and spun about. She gazed all around the back lawn. Whatever had been following her, it was gone now.

Obi leaned up against one of the logs. She was totally stressed out. She was all out of breath, and her poor heart was banging inside her chest. As Obi waited to regain her composure, an idea occurred to her. If she were to climb up to the top of the wood-pile, she'd be able to see far and wide. From the top, she might be able to spot Kenobi! Excited by this idea, Obi turned to scamper up the wood-pile. Before she could begin her ascent, though, a loud, stern voice cried out:

"DON'T MOVE!"

Chapter Sixteen

The Woodpile

The moment she heard someone shout "DON'T MOVE!" Obi let out a loud, startled gasp. Then she did something she probably shouldn't have: she moved. She started to turn to see who had yelled at her.

"I said *DON'T MOVE!*"

Terrified, Obi froze. This time, she didn't move a muscle, not even a whisker.

"Notice the way the light falls upon her head," said the voice, now speaking in a quieter, softer tone. It was the voice of an elderly female creature. Whoever she was, she was standing inside the log cave that Obi was standing just outside of. "See how the light catches the troubled, frightened look on her face."

Obi, confused, frowned. Anxious as Obi was to see who was saying this, she didn't dare sneak a look. She wasn't about to be yelled at again.

"See the way she stands," the voice continued, "with her shoulders stooped."

Hearing this, Obi stood up straighter. Who was this creature and who was she speaking to? Obi heard scratching noises from within the log cave. She thought she recognized the sound. But it couldn't possibly be that. Still, it sure did sound like the scratching noise Rachel made when she sat at her desk, drawing.

"Notice the way her tail curls so your eye is naturally drawn to the front of her body?" the female voice continued.

For several minutes, Obi stood as still as a statue at the mouth of the log cave. She was no longer quite so nervous. She figured that if the creatures who were in the log cave wished to harm her, they would have done so by now.

Obi stood there, half facing the woodpile, half facing the Armstrongs' backyard and the back of the Armstrongs' house. Peering out the corner of her eye, Obi could see Rachel's upstairs bedroom window. Obi wondered if Rachel was awake yet. She must be, Obi decided. She wondered if Rachel had discovered that her little gerbil was missing. Would the girl be as upset about Obi being gone as she had been about Kenobi? What if Rachel didn't miss Obi? What if Rachel didn't even

notice Obi was gone?! What a horrible thing that would be! The very thought brought tears to Obi's eyes.

"Are you crying?" the female voice suddenly said. A small, plump mouse who walked with a cane—well, a twig—limped out of the log cave. She stood in front of Obi and peered into Obi's face. "You *are* crying!"

"Sorry!" Obi apologized. "I'm just a little upset at the moment." She started to lift a front paw to wipe her eyes when she remembered she wasn't supposed to move. "Oh! Sorry, I forgot!" Obi quickly put her paw back down.

"It's okay, you can move now," said the old, plump mouse. She glanced into the log cave and said, "Okay, everyone, wrap it up!" Then, fixing her eyes back on Obi, she said, "So who are you?"

"I'm Obi. I live in the Armstrongs' house."

"Glad to meet you, Obi," said the mouse. "My name is Gertrude. Thank you for modeling for us."

Obi stared at the mouse in astonishment. "I was modeling for you?"

"What do you think?" a cheerful voice asked down by Obi's knees.

Obi looked down and saw a young mouse. He proudly held up a scrap of paper that had scribbles on it.

"This is Bill," said Gertrude.

"Hawo, Bill," said Obi. She studied the scribbles on his scrap of paper. It was a drawing of a stick figure with a big balloon-shaped head, huge fangs, little tiny ears, and paws that looked more like lobster claws than paws. "You drew this?" said Obi, impressed.

Beaming, the little mouse nodded. "It looks just like you, doesn't it?"

"That's *me*?!" cried Obi, horrified. The moment she said it, she was sorry she had. Bill heard the shock in Obi's voice, and his happy face instantly fell. Obi felt bad. She leaned closer to the drawing and, squinting, said, "Why, yes, of course! Now that I look more closely, it does look just like me!"

This cheered Bill right up.

Gertrude placed a paw on Obi's back and said, "Come, I'll introduce you to everyone."

Obi followed Gertrude into the log cave. About a dozen mice were sitting and standing about—young mice, old mice, middle-aged mice, fat mice, skinny mice. Each mouse had a broken piece of a crayon in his or her two front paws. The mice were drawing on little scraps of paper.

"This is the most amazing thing I've ever seen!" said Obi.

Gertrude laughed. "Everyone, this is Obi."

The mice peered up from their drawings and, smiling, said hello to Obi.

"Hawo!" said Obi, and gave them all a little wave.

Gertrude introduced each of the mice to Obi. As Obi followed Gertrude about the log cave, she wondered what it would be like to have your home be in a woodpile. She couldn't imagine herself living in one. The log cave was so dark, so bleak, and, in wintertime, would be so cold. Yet this colony of mice seemed perfectly happy.

"Where did you get all the crayons?" Obi asked.

"From the Armstrong twins," replied Gertrude. "They sometimes leave them outside on their back patio. Hey, finders keepers, losers weepers! As for the scraps of paper, we get them from the Armstrongs' garbage."

Gertrude led Obi over to a big pile of seeds. "Hungry?" she asked.

Obi stared at the pile of seeds in astonishment. She'd never seen so many different kinds of seeds.

"Thanks!" she said as she helped herself to a sunflower seed. "Where did you get all these seeds?"

"From the bird feeder that hangs outside the Armstrongs' kitchen window," replied Gertrude. "The seeds drop down to the grass and we grab them. So tell me, Obi, what brings you to our woodpile?"

"Well," said Obi, "I'm looking for a—"

"DON'T MOVE!" cried Gertrude suddenly.

Obi, who had been about to pop the sunflower seed into her mouth, held her mouth open and her paw frozen in the air.

Gertrude called out to the other mice, "Everyone, come take a look at this!"

The mice hurried over to Gertrude and Obi.

"See how Obi's paw is in the air. Your eye goes straight to the paw and then to her wide-open mouth."

"Nice!" said Bill. He picked up his crayon and began to draw Obi.

"I'm sorry, Obi, you were saying?" Gertrude asked.

Obi took this as a sign that it was okay to move again. She ate the sunflower seed and then said, "I'm looking for a dog."

"What kind of a dog?"

"A little puppy."

"Why are you looking for him?"

Obi hesitated. She wasn't sure how much she should tell Gertrude. She liked Gertrude, and Obi was worried that if she told her the whole sordid story and Obi's less than admirable role in it, Gertrude might not like her. But Obi had done what she had done and, like it or not, she'd have to live with the consequences. Plus, it was hard to tell why Kenobi was lost without explaining *how* he got lost. So Obi told Gertrude everything, even how Obi had let the puppy escape. Obi expected Gertrude to be absolutely horrified at what she had done. But to Obi's surprise, she wasn't. In fact, Gertrude totally understood.

"I would've done the exact same thing," she said.

"You would've?!"

"You were stressed out."

"I *was* stressed out!" Obi agreed. "I was very stressed out!"

"And angry!"

"Yes, I was angry, too!" admitted Obi. "Very, very angry!"

"But don't worry, you'll find the puppy."

"How can you be so sure?"

"Because, Obi, I know which direction you need to go in to find him."

Obi stared at the old mouse. "You do?"

Gertrude nodded. "He came by here yesterday. He sniffed all around our woodpile."

"That sounds like Kenobi!" said Obi. "He's a very curious dog."

"Come," said Gertrude. "I'll show you the direction he took off in."

Obi followed Gertrude to the opening of the cave. Gertrude stepped out onto the end of the log, into the open air and bright sunshine. She pointed her cane at the yellow house that was next door to the Armstrongs'. "He headed that way," she said.

"Well, then, that's where I need to head," said Obi. She turned and gave Gertrude a big hug. "Thank you so much for everything, Gertrude."

"Good luck, Obi," said Gertrude. "If you're ever near our woodpile again, be sure to stop by. You're a great artist's model."

"Oh! Well, thank you," said Obi.

Obi walked out onto the end of the log. She rose up on her hind legs, crouched, and swung her front paws back, like a human diver about to plunge into a swimming pool. Obi was about to leap off the woodpile when Gertrude cried out: "DON'T MOVE!"

Obi froze. Out the corner of her eye, she saw Gertrude turn toward the log cave. "Everyone, come take a look at this."

The other mice hurried out of the log cave and gathered around Gertrude and Obi. Gertrude pointed at Obi. "See the determined look on Obi's face. It's like nothing can stop her!"

"Nice!" cried Bill. He lifted his broken crayon and began to sketch Obi on his scrap of paper.

"Sorry, Bill, you can't draw Obi now," said Gertrude. "She needs to go. This is a gerbil on a mission!" Gertrude turned to Obi and said, "Don't worry, Obi, you'll find that dog. I just know you will."

Gertrude's words had a positive effect on Obi. Feeling extremely confident all of a sudden, Obi leaped off the log. She landed softly on the grass. She turned and peered up at the woodpile.

"Bye, everyone!" shouted Obi, waving to the mice.

The colony of mice all waved back and yelled goodbyes. Then, as if that wasn't nice enough, the mice, clapping their front paws, broke into a spirited chant:

"O-bee! O-bee! O-bee! O-bee!"

Obi, smiling, turned and headed in the direction of the yellow house. The mice's chanting grew fainter and fainter as Obi made her way through the grass. She felt sad to leave the woodpile. She had really enjoyed meeting Gertrude and the other mice. They were all so talented and, well, cheerful. It was nice to know that not all mice were bitter and filled with hate the way Mr. Durkins was. He gave mice such a bad reputation. He really did.

Chapter Seventeen

Jailbreak!

It's amazing what can happen when someone believes in you, and says so, the way Gertrude had said so to Obi. It can really boost your self-confidence and self-esteem. Throw in a bunch of enthusiastic mice perched on a woodpile, chanting out your name and happily cheering you on, and, well, you're all set to go out and conquer the world!

Or, at least, find a lost puppy.

That was how Obi felt as she made her way across the Armstrongs' back lawn toward the next door neighbors' yellow house. There was no doubt in her mind now that she would find Kenobi.

But then, unfortunately, she heard it again.

That strange, rustling sound!

It was back!

Back and sounding as close and as spooky as ever!

"Please go away!" Obi murmured as she picked up her pace.

But the strange, rustling sound did not go away! It kept following her! Obi glanced over her shoulder, but, like before, she saw no creature, just lots of tall, unmowed grass. Obi flicked her gaze back toward the woodpile. Gertrude and the other mice had all gone back into their log cave.

Obi peered in front of her. Up ahead, she spotted the sandbox that the Armstrong twins played in. This gave her an idea. If she ran to the sandbox, she could hide in it and maybe ditch the creature. It was a bit of a long shot, but it wasn't like Obi had many choices here.

Taking a deep breath, Obi took off. She sprinted like a maniac toward the sandbox and leaped into a sand pail that lay in the grass.

Over the wild pounding of her heart, Obi heard the strange, rustling sound grow louder as the creature grew closer. Obi closed her eyes and waited, hoping the creature had not seen her duck into the pail. She heard the creature race up to the sandbox.

Then she heard it go right past the sand pail!

Obi peeked out from inside the pail. In the tall grass, she spotted a gray fluffy tail bouncing about in the air, twitching uncontrollably. It was the tail of a—

Oh, no!

It wasn't!

It *was!* It was that goofball squirrel who lived in the Norway maple—the one who was convinced that Obi was a criminal because she lived in a cage.

Obi, fuming, leaped out from behind the pail.

"You!" she cried, pointing an accusatory paw at the squirrel.

The squirrel let out a shriek. He spun about. He looked terrified.

"Please don't hurt me!" he cried, throwing up his front paws in surrender.

"Why have you been following me?" Obi demanded.

"I was curious to see what a criminal does after a jailbreak."

"Jailbreak? What are you talking about?"

"Don't worry!" said the squirrel. "Your secret is safe with me! I won't tell anyone that you've broken out of jail!"

"Look, how many times do I have to tell you?" said Obi. "I'm *not* a criminal!"

"Then why do you live in a jail?"

"It's not a jail! It's my cage!"

Obi sighed in exasperation. She didn't have time for this! She really didn't! She had a puppy to find!

"I don't have time for this!" cried Obi. And with that, she continued on her way.

The squirrel hurried to catch up with Obi.

"Where are you going now?" he asked. "You're not planning on breaking into the next door neighbors' house, are you?"

"Of course not!" replied Obi.

"Are you going to steal their human mobile?"

"NO!" cried Obi. She suddenly realized something and stopped. She glared at the squirrel and said, "What are you doing?"

The squirrel stopped. He looked very frightened. "Nothing," he replied.

"You're tagging along after me!" cried Obi. "I don't want you tagging along after me!"

"But I want to find out what a criminal does after a jailbreak!"

"How many times do I have to tell you?" said Obi, losing her temper. "I'm *NOT* a criminal! And I haven't broken out of jail!"

"Then what are you doing out here?"

"Look, if you must know, I'm searching for a little dog."

"Why?" asked the squirrel. "Did he double-cross you? Are you trying to get even with him?"

"No, he didn't double-cross me and no, I'm not trying to get even with him!" said Obi. "The dog is lost and I'm trying to find him!"

"He must've done something!" insisted the squirrel.

"He didn't!" said Obi.

"C'mon, you can tell me!" said the squirrel. "What did he do?"

"He didn't do anything!"

A few things about this squirrel were quickly becoming clear to Obi: 1) He really was totally daft in the head. 2) He was going to keep tagging along whether Obi wanted him to or not. 3) He didn't want to hear the truth—he only wanted to hear what *he* wanted to hear.

So Obi decided to give him what he wanted.

"Okay, I'll level with you," said Obi. "I really am a criminal."

"I knew it!" cried the squirrel.

"But I'm not the kind of criminal you think I am."

"What kind are you?"

"Well . . . . have you ever heard of Robin Hood?"

The squirrel shook his head. This didn't surprise Obi. Why would *he* have heard of Robin Hood, the noble outlaw of the Middle Ages who robbed from the rich and gave to the poor? The squirrel didn't get to listen to bedtime stories the way Obi did when Mr. Armstrong read to Rachel at night before she went to sleep. That was how Obi had heard of Robin Hood and his Sherwood Forest gang. It saddened Obi to remember how Mr. Armstrong read stories aloud to Rachel. It made her yearn for the good old days. Obi felt so lucky she got to hear stories. The squirrel never got to hear stories. That made Obi feel a little sorry for the squirrel.

"Anyway, I'm like Robin Hood," continued Obi. "I'm a criminal but I have a kind heart. I steal from the rich and give to the poor. I've got a gang that helps me. One of the gang members is this dog. But he got lost. That's why I had to break out of my cage—I mean, my jail. I have to go find him."

"What about your little friend?" asked the squirrel. "Is he looking for the dog, too?"

Obi frowned. "Little friend? What little friend?"

"You know, that little mouse I saw up in the Armstrongs' attic with you."

"Oh, you mean Mr. Dur-kins!" said Obi. "No, he's not looking for the dog. He's back

in the Armstrongs' house, guarding the hideout."

As Obi said this, something else occurred to her.

Maybe this squirrel, as nutty as he was, might be able to help her find Kenobi.

"You know," said Obi, "I could use someone like you in my gang!"

"Oh, no!" said the squirrel, eyes wide, vehemently shaking his head. "Not me! I don't want to be a criminal! I don't want to end up like my Uncle Leroy! I don't want to end up in a trap and never be seen or heard from again!"

Obi knew all about Uncle Leroy. The squirrel had once told Obi about how his Uncle Leroy had been captured in a trap that Mr. Armstrong had set in the shrubs outside the Armstrongs' house. Fortunately, it was the kind of trap that captured the animal alive and didn't hurt or kill him. Mr. Armstrong had taken Uncle Leroy someplace far away. Nobody had ever seen or heard from him again.

"Don't worry," said Obi, "you're not going to end up like your Uncle Leroy."

"How do you know?"

"Because I look out for my friends! I don't let bad things happen to them!"

The squirrel thought about this for a moment. Then he said, "So what do you want me to do?"

"Well, I've been watching you," said Obi. "I'm very impressed at how well you climb up telephone poles and run across telephone wires."

"Well, I am a squirrel," he said modestly.

"See that telephone pole?" Obi pointed to a telephone pole that stood on the front lawn of the next door neighbors' property, by the street. Obi and the squirrel were on the side lawn of the Armstrongs' house, between the Armstrongs' lawn and the next door neighbors' house. "I need you to climb up it and look around and tell me if you see a little puppy that looks like he's lost."

"Sure, I can do that!" said the squirrel.

"Then let's go do it!"

Obi and the squirrel hurried over to the telephone pole. The squirrel leaped up onto the pole and fearlessly scampered up the side of it. He was an amazing climber! He made it to the top of the pole in a matter of seconds!

To see the squirrel, Obi had to tilt her head way back. "See anything?" she called out.

The squirrel scanned the horizon. "No sign of a puppy anywhere!" he yelled back.

"Try the telephone wire!" Obi shouted. "Maybe you'll see him from there!"

The squirrel jumped onto the telephone wire.

Tail bouncing, he began running across it. To get a better of the view of the squirrel, Obi moved to the other side of the telephone pole. As she lifted her eyes upward, she saw the poster.

It was about five feet from the ground and stapled onto the brown telephone pole. The poster showed a photograph of a little puppy's cute face. Obi stared at the photo, incredulous. It was Kenobi! Above the photograph, in big, bold, black capital letters, the poster said:

Obi wondered who had put the poster up there. Probably Mr. Armstrong, she decided. Or Rachel. Or both of them. Obi began to read the poster. She was reading the part about where to call if you should find the puppy when she felt something wet plop down upon her left shoulder. Obi, bewildered, glanced at her shoulder and saw a glop of slimy, disgusting slobber!

Someone had just drooled on her!

Obi wiped the slobber off her shoulder and looked up. She nearly fainted from shock. A huge black Newfoundland dog was hovering above her. Head tilted back, he, too, was reading the poster on the telephone pole.

"Want me to tell you what it says?" the enormous dog asked.

"Excuse me?" said Obi. It made her nervous being so close to such a big dog.

"This poster," said the Newfoundland. "Want me to tell you what it says? It says 'Pancake Breakfast at My House! All Welcome!'"

Obi, puzzled, shifted her eyes from the dog to the poster. She frowned. Were she and this big black Newfoundland reading the same poster?

"That's not what it says," said Obi.

"Yes, it does!" said the Newfoundland.

"No, it doesn't!"

"Yes, it does!"

"No," said Obi. "It does not."

"Then what does it say?"

"It says 'Lost Puppy! Reward!'"

The Newfoundland chuckled. He looked terribly amused. "It does not say that!"

"It does so!" insisted Obi.

"Okay, then, what else does the poster say?"

"It says, 'Lost golden retriever puppy. Answers to the name Kenobi. $50 reward for anyone who finds Kenobi. Please call—'"

"Wow! You're good!" interrupted the Newfoundland. "How can you make this stuff up so fast?"

"I'm not making it up!" cried Obi, insulted. "That's what the poster says!"

"And how, may I ask, do you know that?"

"Because I can read, that's how!" Obi had never confessed this to anyone. It was one of her most intimate secrets.

The Newfoundland chuckled. "A gerbil that can read!" he said. "That's fabulous!"

"But I can!" exclaimed Obi. As Obi was saying this, she spotted the squirrel. He was climbing, headfirst, down the telephone pole. The moment the squirrel saw the Newfoundland, he stopped in his tracks. His eyes widened with alarm and then he spun about and hurried back up the pole.

The Newfoundland, whose gaze was on Obi the whole time, had not noticed the squirrel. "Okay, smarty, what's my dog tag say?"

The Newfoundland lay down on the grass and lowered his head so Obi could read the dog tag that hung from his collar.

Obi clasped the small, shiny, round metal tag in her two front paws. She had to move a tuft of thick black fur aside so she could see what was etched on the tag.

"'My name is Mookie,'" she read out loud. "'I belong to—'"

"Whoa!" cried the Newfoundland. He sounded shocked. His head snapped up, causing the dog tag to rip out of Obi's paws. The dog stared at Obi in amazement. "You really can read!"

"I told you!" said Obi.

"Who taught you how to read?"

"Nobody taught me. I learned it on my own."

"This is incredible! Do you know what the odds are of a gerbil knowing how to read?"

"No, what?" asked Obi, who was extremely interested to find out.

Either the dog didn't know, or like Kenobi, he had an infuriatingly short attention span, for he abruptly changed the subject. He narrowed his eyes suspiciously at Obi and said, "So why are you so interested in this puppy?"

"He belongs to my adoptive mother," replied Obi. "She misses him dearly. That's why I'm trying to find him."

"You're sure it's not because of the reward money?"

Obi stared at the Newfoundland. She couldn't believe he would think such a thing about her. "No! Absolutely not!"

Apparently, though, the Newfoundland did not believe Obi. "Tell you what," he said. "I'll make a deal with you. If you split the reward money with me, I'll tell you what I know about this puppy."

"You know something about him?" asked Obi.

"I sure do," said the Newfoundland. "I ran into him yesterday. I gave him some good advice. So what do you say? Will you go halfsies with me on the reward?"

"You can have all the reward money," replied Obi. "I

just want to find this puppy. So what advice did you give him?"

The Newfoundland was about to say something when, down the street, a woman's voice called out: "Moooookie!"

The Newfoundland's head jerked in the direction of the woman's voice. "That's my owner!" he exclaimed excitedly. "Wonder what she wants?"

"Mookie! Come, Mookie!" the woman's voice called out.

"I've got to go!" cried the Newfoundland.

"Wait!" cried Obi. "Before you go, what did you say to the puppy?"

"Moooookeee! Come, Moooookeee!" cried the woman's voice.

The Newfoundland looked very anxious as well as confused about what he should do—stay and talk to Obi or obey his owner. "I've got to go see what my owner wants!"

"First tell me what you said to the puppy!" said Obi. "Please, Mookie, I've got to know!"

"I told him not to go anywhere near Rex!" replied the Newfoundland.

"Rex? Who's Rex?"

"He's the German shepherd who lives in the brown house at the end of the street."

"What's wrong with Rex?"

"He's a really mean dog!" explained the Newfoundland. "He'll bite you if you're not careful! So I told the puppy not to go anywhere near Rex's house. And that's my advice to you, too. If you know what's good for you, little gerbil, don't go anywhere near Rex!"

"Don't worry, I won't!" said Obi. "Thanks for telling me!"

"Mooooooookeeeeeee!" the woman's voice called out again.

Obi watched as the Newfoundland, barking, bounded down the street.

Now that the Newfoundland was gone, the squirrel came back down the telephone pole. With a leap, he landed beside Obi.

"I don't like that dog!" he said to Obi. "He's always chasing me! He's not part of your gang, is he?"

"*Him?* No way!" said Obi. "So did you see any sign of the puppy from the telephone wire?"

"Nothing," replied the squirrel. "So what do we do now?"

Obi sighed. She honestly did not know. "I don't know," she confessed, "but I'll tell you one thing. I'm not going anywhere near the brown house that's at the end of this street. I just found out there's a really mean dog that lives there."

Obi heard herself say this and realized something.

"Yes, of course, he would!" she exclaimed. Excited, Obi broke into a run.

"Where are you going?" asked the squirrel.

"I know where to find the puppy!" Obi shouted over her shoulder.

Chapter Nineteen

The Really Mean Dog

Obi raced across one front lawn, then another. She knew just where to go: to the brown house at the end of the street.

Yes, the brown house where the really mean dog lived.

Even though Obi had been warned by the Newfoundland not to go there, she knew this was where she'd find Kenobi. He *had* to be there. Whenever Obi had told Kenobi not to do something, what had the puppy done? Exactly what Obi had told him *not* to do! The Newfoundland said he had told Kenobi not to go anywhere near the brown house where the really mean dog lived. Obi could just see the puppy hearing this and then, lickety-split, making a beeline for the brown house.

Even if Obi hadn't known that the brown house was at the end of the street, she would have had no trouble finding it. All she needed to do was follow the sound of a dog's ferocious barking. The barking came from behind the brown house. With the squirrel tagging along, Obi hurried around to the back of the house, slipped under a hydrangea bush, and peeked out. A German shepherd stood near the edge of the woods, barking at something there.

Obi was shocked. You'd think a family that owned a really mean dog would keep the dog fenced in or, at the very least, tied up. But they didn't! The really mean dog was roaming around the backyard free as a bird!

"Is this the dog you're looking for?" asked the squirrel. His voice quivered as he, too, peeked out from the bush. The squirrel's fluffy tail was twitching nervously all over the place.

"No, he's not the dog," replied Obi. "But I think he knows where the dog I'm looking for is."

"How are you going to find out?"

Obi wasn't really sure. "I guess I'll have to ask him."

The squirrel looked horrified. "Y-you're going to *talk* to him?!"

"I have no choice," replied Obi. "I *have* to find Kenobi."

Obi decided to wait until the dog calmed down a bit before venturing over to talk to him. The only problem was, the German shepherd did *not* calm down! He just kept barking and barking! An hour passed. Then another hour. Then several more hours passed.

The dog kept barking into the woods. Every once in a while, the dog's owner would stick her head out the back door of the house and yell out, "Quiet, Rex!"

The German shepherd would lie down and stop barking then, whereupon Obi would start to head over to him. But then, the darn dog would leap up and start barking wildly again into the woods, and Obi, all atremble, would rush back to under the hydrangea bush, where the squirrel, looking scared stiff, was cowering.

Finally, by the end of the day, Obi realized she had to do something. She couldn't just sit there waiting. She had to take her chances. And so, with her heart beating hard, Obi stepped out from under the hydrangea bush. She was absolutely terrified as she made her way across the back lawn toward the barking German shepherd. Who knew what this really mean dog might do to Obi? Tear her from limb to limb? Swallow her up in a single bite? Obi tried not to think about it. She was on a mission, she told herself. She had a puppy to find and nothing, not even a really mean German shepherd, was going to stop her!

At least that's what she kept telling herself.

Obi walked right up behind the barking German shepherd and halted. Her whole body was quivering with fear.

"Hawo!" she said in her most friendly voice.

The dog was barking so fiercely loud, he didn't hear Obi. Indeed, Obi could scarcely hear herself.

"HAWO!" she said again, only much louder this time. *That* got his attention. The dog stopped barking and whirled about, startled.

"Sorry! Didn't mean to startle you!" said Obi quickly. The dog's face instantly darkened. He narrowed his eyes at Obi and let out a ferocious growl. "Ah-ha!" he snarled. "Caught you in the act!" Obi had no idea what the dog was talking about.

"I beg your pardon?" she said.

"Don't play innocent with me, Missy!" the German shepherd said. "I'm onto you!"

"You are?"

"I must admit, I wasn't expecting you to be a little mouse."

"Well, actually, I'm not a little mouse," said Obi. "I'm a little gerbil."

"So what did you do with it?" the dog demanded.

"What did I do with what?"

"You know perfectly well with what! With my rubber ball! What did you do with it?"

"I didn't do anything with it!"

"You stole it!"

"I did not!"

"Don't deny it!" barked the German shepherd. "You're a doggy-toy stealer!"

"I am *not* a doggy-toy stealer!"

"Oh, like I'm supposed to believe that?"

"As a matter of fact, yes!" replied Obi. "What would I, a little gerbil, want with one of your doggy toys?"

The German shepherd was quiet for a moment as he pondered this. He must have thought Obi had made a good point, for he said, "If you're not here to steal one of my doggy toys, why are you here?"

"I'm here to ask you if you've seen a little puppy," replied Obi.

"No, I have not!" replied the German shepherd.

"Are you sure?" said Obi. "I'm almost certain he came here."

"Well, I haven't seen him!" snapped the German shepherd. "Unless . . ." His voice trailed off.

"Unless what?" asked Obi.

"*Unless* he's the one in the woods."

"Someone is in the woods?"

"I keep hearing noises in the woods."

Obi thought about this for a moment. Could it be Kenobi?

"That might be him!" she said. "Thanks for telling me about this!"

Obi started for the woods. She'd taken only a couple of steps, though, when she heard a vicious snarl. She peered up. The German shepherd was glowering at her with the most menacing look in his eyes. "And where do you think you're going?" he demanded.

"Oh! Um, well . . . to the woods," replied Obi. "I want to go see if those noises you're hearing are being made by the puppy I'm looking for."

"I don't think so!" said the German shepherd.

"You don't think what?"

"I don't think you're going anywhere!"

Obi gulped. "You don't?"

The dog shook his head. "Nope, I don't. You know what I do think?"

Obi shook her head.

"I think whoever is in the woods took my favorite rubber ball and that *you* helped him steal it. *That's* why you're here! You're hoping to distract me so whoever is in the woods can come out and steal another one of my doggy toys!"

Obi did not like where this conversation was going. The German shepherd was angry and he didn't seem to be too bright, and, well, frankly, those two things do not make a good combination. Particularly for a little gerbil who's in the same backyard with a really mean dog.

Obi tried to remain calm. *Think, Obi, think!* she said to herself. *How do I get out of this mess?*

And then, despite being all but paralyzed with fear, Obi thought of something.

"Don't come out yet!" she shouted, waving her two front paws as if she was signaling to someone in the woods. "He's onto us!"

The German shepherd swung around and, barking fiercely, rushed over to the edge of the woods.

Obi hadn't really seen anyone. She had just shouted

this out to distract the dog. The moment the German shepherd took his eyes off Obi, the gerbil spun around and ran like crazy for the woods. The dog saw Obi escaping. At that point, he must have put two and two together and realized he had been tricked. He became absolutely furious! Barking insanely, he charged at Obi, with a fiery look in his dark eyes.

Obi shrieked. She heard an even louder shriek right beside her. It came from the squirrel; he had come out of hiding to join Obi.

"HEAD FOR THE WOODS!" Obi shouted to the squirrel.

As Obi and the squirrel sprinted into the woods, Obi heard a strange sound behind them. At first, she thought it was the really mean dog chasing after them. But to Obi's surprise, the German shepherd had mysteriously stopped short at the edge of the woods.

Okay, so if the really mean dog wasn't behind them, who was? The noise sounded like—Obi gasped when she realized what it sounded like.

The noise sounded like wings. Beating wings! Furiously beating wings!

Terrified, Obi glanced back over her shoulder. An enormous bird with an impressive wingspan and enormous, piercing eyes that almost seemed to glow was flying down from the sky, heading straight toward *her*!

It was an owl!

Obi ran even faster. She heard the rushing sound of the owl's wings grow louder. Suddenly, Obi felt something sharp dig into the fur on her back. The owl had grabbed Obi with his talons.

"Aaaahhhhhhhh!" shrieked Obi.

The next thing Obi knew, she was being lifted up into the air!

Chapter Twenty The Owl

Obi had never been so terrified in all her life. As the owl whisked her away, she glanced down and saw the squirrel on the ground, with his face tilted up, a horrified look in his eyes.

"Quick, Squirrel!" yelled Obi. "Go get help!"

Obi wasn't really counting on the squirrel to go get help. After all, who would he get help from? The really mean dog? Obi had just said this so the owl would hear her and think the squirrel was going to return with a rescue party—or better yet, a huge army—that would stop at nothing to free Obi. If the owl thought reinforcements were on the way, maybe, just maybe, he'd let Obi go.

But, alas, that did not happen. The owl kept flying over the treetops, with Obi dangling in his sharp claws.

If Obi hadn't been so horribly frightened and if the owl's claws hadn't hurt quite so much, she might have enjoyed being up in the air, with a bird's-eye view of her neighborhood. For another, it would have allowed Obi to search for Kenobi from high up in the air.

But Obi was much too stressed out to enjoy her first flying experience. As for looking for Kenobi, the light was fading fast and the woods below were a gray smudge. A little puppy would be all but impossible to spot.

Obi peered ahead and saw that the owl was flying toward an old, leafless, gnarled tree that stood rather spookily in the dark, shadow-filled forest. With Obi still clutched in her claws, the owl sailed into a small hole in the trunk of the tree, about twenty feet up from the ground. In the dimly lit hole, the owl released Obi. He then perched himself in front of the hole so Obi would be unable to escape.

"What are you going to do with me?" cried Obi. She was hysterical, she was so frightened. "Why did you bring me here? Where are we? How long are you going to keep me? Is there anything I can do to persuade you to let me go?"

"Look, I've had a really hard day, okay?" snapped the owl irritably. "I'm tired and I have no patience for a lot of idle chitchat!"

"Oh, sorry!" said Obi. "I didn't know."

"Yeah, well, now you know," grumbled the owl.

Obi decided that, since the owl didn't want to hear any small talk, she should just get right to the point.

"You're not going to . . ."

But Obi found that she was unable to say what she was terrified the owl was going to do to her. It was just too horrible to say out loud.

"I'm not going to *what*?" demanded the owl in a very peevish voice, glaring at Obi. Even though it was dark as anything inside the hole, Obi could see the owl's two green, piercing eyes focused upon her. The owl's eyes almost glowed! It was very eerie!

"You know . . ." said Obi, still unable to say the words.

"No, I don't know!" cried the owl impatiently. "What do I look like? A mind reader?"

He certainly was an ill-tempered owl!

But Obi tried once again to finish her question. "I was just wondering, if, well, you know, if you were going to . . . um . . . you know . . . um . . . eat me." Obi said "eat me" in the tiniest of tiny voices.

"Well, *duh!*" said the owl. "Why did you think I brought you here? To chat?"

"Well, no," said Obi, feeling a bit stupid.

"Yes, of course, I'm going to—" The owl suddenly stopped talking and made a pained face. *"Oh, no!"* he groaned. "There he goes again!"

"There *who* goes again?" asked Obi.

"That dog!" exclaimed the owl. "That infuriating, idiotic, wretched, inconsiderate dog! All he does all day is bark, bark, bark!"

Now that the owl mentioned it, Obi did hear a lot of barking off in the distance. It was coming from the direction of the brown house where the German shepherd lived.

"Ugh!" cried the owl. "That incessant barking is driving me nuts! Nuts! Nuts! *NUTS!* Doesn't that dog know owls sleep during the day and hunt at night!?"

"I guess not," said Obi.

"How am I supposed to get any sleep during the day when he barks and barks and barks? I can't! And I can't sleep at night because I'm programmed to stay up and hunt!"

"I can see where that could be a problem," said Obi.

"I haven't had a decent sleep in two days!" cried the owl. "Every time I start to fall asleep, that infernal dog starts barking! Look at me! I'm a nervous wreck! My nerves are all shot!" The owl peered out his hole into the dark woods and said, "What on earth is that dog barking at now?"

Obi had a pretty good idea what the German shepherd was barking at: her. Before running off into the woods, Obi had whipped the dog up into a frenzy. He was probably still standing at the edge of his backyard, barking into the shadowy woods. Obi decided it was best not to tell the owl this, though.

"I have no idea what he could be barking at," she said.

"He's been barking like this since yesterday morning!"

"Oh, really?" said Obi, surprised. "Since yesterday morning?"

"What would cause a dog to bark for so long?" the owl asked.

Obi thought she knew. And it wasn't because of Obi. How could it be? The really mean dog hadn't even known Obi existed until about a half hour ago. Kenobi had run away yesterday morning. Could it be the really mean dog was barking at Kenobi?

"I can't stand it, I tell you, I can't stand it!" cried the owl, becoming more and more agitated. He was unraveling before Obi's very eyes. "I need *SLEEP*!"

And then the owl did a very unexpected thing. He

spun around and, to Obi's horror, stuck

RUFF!

RUFF!

RUFF!

his head out the hole and began to bark like a crazy dog into the darkness.

"Ruff! Ruff! Ruff!"

The owl was making Obi very, very nervous. She didn't know a lot about owls, but she was pretty sure that barking like a dog was not normal owl behavior. What little Obi did know about owls she had learned from the books that Mr. Armstrong read to Rachel at bedtime. Obi's favorite owl book was *Sam and the Firefly*.

The owl in the story was named Sam. He was a kind and understanding owl and he did not bark like a dog.

"Gosh, you're not at all like Sam!" Obi heard herself blurt out loud.

The owl stopped barking and pulled his head back into the hole. He glowered at Obi and said, "Who's Sam?"

"You know," said Obi. "From the story *Sam and the Firefly.*"

"No, I don't know!" said the owl. "Tell it to me!"

"Oh! Okay! Sure, I'd be happy to!" said Obi.

And so Obi told the story about Sam and the firefly to

the owl. She found she rather enjoyed telling the story. It took her mind off her hopeless situation. While Obi told the story, she couldn't help noticing the magical effect it seemed to have on the owl. His eyes softened and he looked totally engrossed. Better still, the story seemed to mollify him. He seemed less jittery, more gentle. When Obi finished the story, the owl said, "That was a good story! Know any others?"

"Actually, I do!" said Obi excitedly. "I know lots of them!" Which, in fact, was true. Mr. Armstrong had read lots and lots of bedtime stories to Rachel. They were all in Obi's head, like a huge library.

"Well, then, tell me another!" ordered the owl.

Obi wondered what story to tell next. Since the owl liked *Sam and the Firefly* so much, Obi thought he might also like *A Fly Went By,* since they were similar in that they were both short and had happy endings. So Obi began telling the story of *A Fly Went By.* She hadn't gotten very far into the story, though, when the owl rather rudely interrupted her.

"When do we get to the owl part?" he demanded.

"The owl part?" said Obi. "There's no owl in this story."

"What do you mean there's no *owl*?!" cried the owl. He looked annoyed. "Why are you telling it to me, then?"

"You said you wanted to hear a good story," said Obi.

"I said a good *owl* story," said the owl.

Obi shook her head. "No, you didn't."

"Yes, I did!"

"No, I'm sorry, but you didn't," said Obi. "You simply said you wanted to hear another good story. You didn't say anything about an owl story."

"I most certainly did!" insisted the owl, becoming irritable again. "Don't tell me what I did or didn't say! I said I wanted a good owl story! Now tell me one!"

"Okay, okay!" said Obi, holding up her front paws. Meanwhile, she was thinking, *Geez, what a hothead!*

Obi quickly tried to think of an owl story. A couple came to mind: *The Owl and the Pussycat* and *Winnie-the-Pooh*. The thing was, though, you had to be in the right mood to tell a certain type of story. There were many times when Mr. Armstrong was going to read to Rachel and one of them would suggest a book, but the other one would say he or she wasn't in the mood for that kind of a story that night. Obi felt the same way about these two stories. She wanted to tell a story that was a bit more exciting, something that would cause the owl's heart to pound fast and that would keep him on the edge of his nest. Suddenly, Obi knew just what story to tell.

"I'll tell you about Harry Potter!"

"Is he an owl?"

"No," said Obi, "but he has a pet owl named Hedwig." Before the owl could ask another question, Obi jumped into telling the story of *Harry Potter and the Sorcerer's Stone*.

She was halfway into what would have been the second chapter if she'd actually been reading the book aloud when Obi heard a snore. She stopped telling the story and stared at the owl. His eyes were closed, and his chin was resting on his feathery chest. The owl had fallen asleep! Obi couldn't believe it! How could the owl fall asleep during a Harry Potter story?! It was unheard of!

"Hey, what are you doing?" cried Obi, annoyed. "Wake up!" She reached over and poked the owl in the chest with her front paw.

The owl's eyes jerked open. For a moment, he seemed to be in a daze. He gaped at Obi like he wasn't quite sure what this gerbil was doing in his nest.

"You fell asleep!" said Obi. "Don't fall asleep! This is a really good story!"

"Sorry," said the owl, yawning. "Just so . . . so . . . sleepy. Haven't slept in days. Need sleep . . ."

Obi saw the owl's eyelids growing heavier and heavier.

"Wake up!" exclaimed Obi, and poked the owl again.

The owl opened his eyes wide and said, "I'm awake! Keep telling the story!"

Obi picked up where she had left off. She was at the part where Harry arrives at Hogwarts when suddenly she heard another snore.

The owl had fallen asleep again!

Chapter Twenty-one Lions and Tigers and What's That?!

Obi stood on her hind legs and put her front paws on her hips. She frowned at the owl and gave him her most disdainful look. How could he fall asleep while listening to a story? Obi never fell asleep when Mr. Armstrong read stories aloud to Rachel! Nor, for that matter, did Rachel! And to think the owl had nodded off during a spellbinding Harry Potter story! What would J. K. Rowling say? She wouldn't have been very happy, that was for sure.

Obi sighed and leaned forward to wake the owl up again. Then she realized something and quickly pulled her paw back.

What was she thinking!? This was a perfect opportunity for her to escape!

Obi silently crept over to the sleeping owl. He was still blocking the entrance of the hole, so Obi had to be very quiet and cautious. Her heart pounded wildly as she moved close to the owl. Holding her breath, Obi squeezed past the owl and stuck her head out the hole. Glancing down, she saw how high up she was, and gasped. It scared her to be up so high. If only she were that goofy squirrel, she could just scamper down the side of the tree.

C'mon, Obi, you can do this, Obi told herself. When the Armstrongs went on vacation, who was able to fend for herself and get food and water? Obi, of course! She was *Obi, Jedi gerbil*! If she had been able to do that, she could certainly do *this*! But how? As Obi studied the tree, she began to think she might have an idea of how she could get down to the ground without breaking her neck.

Obi climbed out onto the rim of the tree hole. Gathering up all her courage, she leaped to the branch that was just below the hole. As she dropped down, she did a little somersault in midair. She didn't need to do this, but she did. She couldn't resist. It was a Jedi knight thing. From that branch, Obi jumped to the next lower branch. Then to the branch below that. And then the one below that. It wasn't long before Obi was able to drop to the ground without hurting herself.

The moment Obi was on the ground again, she was off. She blindly raced through the dark woods. Only when she had put a good distance between her and the old, dead tree where the owl lived did Obi allow herself to slow down to a walk.

Having escaped from the owl, Obi now found she had another problem: she had no idea where to go. The woods were dark and creepy and filled with strange, spooky shadows and crickets chirping loudly. Obi remembered a movie on TV she had once watched with Rachel. At one point during the movie, a human girl, a scarecrow, a tin man, and a cowardly lion were walking through a dark, creepy forest just like this one. To comfort themselves, they began to say a little chant. Hoping it might comfort her, Obi began to say it, too.

"Lions and tigers and bears, oh my!" Obi said softly to herself as she walked through the dark woods, glancing nervously about. "Lions and tigers and bears, oh my! Lions and tigers and *what's that*?!"

Something was rushing up behind her! Obi didn't need to look to see what it was. She knew. It was the owl! Obviously, he had woken up, found her gone, become furious, and flown in a rage out of his hole to find Obi and bring her back.

Well, he had found her!

Obi sprinted as fast as her legs would go. She heard the owl behind her, catching up. He was getting closer and closer. Sprinting faster, Obi closed her eyes and waited for the owl's razor-sharp talons to dig into her furry back and lift her up into the air.

Then it happened.

But to Obi's astonishment, the owl didn't snatch Obi up in his claws.

No—instead, he tackled her!

The owl fell on top of Obi and practically smothered her. To Obi's surprise and bewilderment, the owl did not feel soft and feathery, but soft and, well, *furry.* Obi felt something wet slap across her face.

Did the owl just *lick* her?!

Obi, confused, opened her eyes and found herself staring into the happy face of—

"Kenobi!" cried Obi in surprise.

The puppy was all over Obi. He wagged his tail and licked Obi over and over again. Obi laughed. She was

absolutely delighted to see the lost puppy. "I am so happy to see you again, Kenobi!" she said. It surprised Obi that she should be so glad to see him, considering how miserable he had made her life, but it was the honest truth—she really was happy to see Kenobi again.

Clearly, from all the licks Obi was receiving, the puppy was just as happy to see the gerbil.

"Where have you been?" Obi asked.

"I've been so scared!" replied the puppy.

"Well, you don't have to be scared anymore," said Obi. "I'm here now!"

"I want to go home, Obi! I want to see Rachel! I miss Rachel!"

"I miss Rachel, too," said Obi. "And don't you worry, we're going home. That's why I'm here—to take you home."

"I don't like these woods! They're scary!" said Kenobi. "How do we get out of here?"

It was a good question. How were they supposed to get out of these dark, creepy woods? Having been flown in, Obi had no idea. Obi decided it was probably best not to tell the puppy this, though. Not after she had told Kenobi he didn't need to be scared because Obi was here now. Obi racked her brain trying to think how they were going to get out of these woods.

"Okay, here's what we're going to do," said Obi. "We're going to sleep in the woods tonight and wait for morning, when it'll be daylight and we'll be able to see how to get out of the woods."

And so the two of them lay down on the ground, beside a log, to go to sleep.

"Listen, Kenobi, there's something I need to tell you," said Obi. "I'm sorry you got lost. It was all my—"

"What was *that*?" asked the puppy, jerking his head up in alarm.

"What was *what*?" asked Obi.

"I thought I heard something!"

Obi glanced warily about the dark woods. "I didn't hear anything. I mean, except for all the crickets. Are you sure you heard something?"

"I thought I was sure," said Kenobi. "But maybe I wasn't so sure."

"Oh. Well, I'm sure it was nothing," said Obi. "So, anyway, as I was saying, Kenobi, it's all my fault that you got lost. I never should have—"

"*There!* Hear *it*?"

"Hear *what*?"

"*That!*"

"I don't hear anything!"

"I thought I heard something!" said the puppy. "You sure you didn't hear anything?"

"I'm pretty sure," said Obi.

"I thought I heard something!" said Kenobi. "But maybe I didn't hear something!"

Obi frowned at Kenobi's shadowy form lying beside her. It was hard to apologize to a dog who kept interrupting you because he thought he was hearing things.

"Well, anyway," said Obi, "I never should have let you out of the house by yourself. I don't know what I was think—"

"Obi, I'm scared!" whimpered Kenobi. "I keep hearing noises! Scary noises!"

Obi tried to think of what she could do. "Tell you what," she said. "How about I tell you a bedtime story?"

"Will it make me feel better?"

"It might!"

"Okay, then," said Kenobi. "Tell me a bedtime story."

Obi tried to think of a good story to tell Kenobi. Harry Potter was definitely out—that would be too scary for a frightened puppy. Obi remembered how the owl had only wanted to hear an owl story. This made Obi think that maybe she should tell a dog story.

"This story is called *Go, Dog, Go!*" said Obi.

"That sounds like a good story!" said Kenobi.

"It *is* a good story!" said Obi.

And so, for the third time that evening, Obi started telling a story that Mr. Armstrong had once read aloud to Rachel. As Obi told the story, Kenobi cuddled up close to the little gerbil, just the way Rachel liked to cuddle up close to her father when he was reading. Obi found she rather liked the puppy cuddling up close to her—it gave her a nice, warm, cozy feeling. At one point, without thinking, Obi started to put her arm around the dog just the way Mr. Armstrong did sometimes to Rachel when he was reading. Realizing what she was doing, Obi stopped, with her paw in midair. Two days ago, she had been all set to throttle this puppy. Now here she was about to put a comforting paw on him! To her surprise, Kenobi moved in closer to her.

Obi was nearly at the end of the story when, glancing into the puppy's face, she saw that his eyes had closed and that he had dozed off.

Obi did not mind that the puppy had drifted off to sleep the way she had been with the owl. It meant that Obi had the ability to tell a story that could comfort a terribly frightened puppy—comfort him where he felt safe enough to drift off to sleep.

Obi lay back against the puppy's soft, warm, furry body and peered up through the gaps in the tree branches and into the starry night. Obi couldn't wait for tomorrow. She couldn't wait to see Rachel's startled but delighted face when she saw Kenobi and Obi return home. Obi wondered if her adoptive mother would realize that Obi had found the lost puppy and brought him home. She sure hoped so. Not that Obi was hoping to get the $50 reward money. No, Obi simply wanted Rachel to be as thrilled to see Obi again as she knew Rachel would be to see Kenobi.

If such a thing were to happen, well, that, to Obi, would be the best reward of all.

Chapter Twenty-two

The Rubber Ball

Obi had the worst time falling asleep. Which wasn't surprising, really, considering how wound up she was from all the excitement of that day. It was also not surprising that, when Obi did finally drift off to sleep, she fell into a deep slumber.

Obi slept so soundly that, she might have slept late into the next morning if the bright morning sun hadn't shone in her sleeping face—and had not someone licked her face.

Obi woke up with a start. Her eyes flew open. Kenobi's big, cheerful puppy face was hovering above the little gerbil, staring down at her.

"Wake up!" the puppy said. "We need to go home! We need to go back to Rachel!"

"Oh, yeah, right!" said Obi, still a bit groggy. She got to her feet and said, "Let's go!"

"Which way do we go?" asked Kenobi.

Obi stood on her hind legs and glanced around the woods. Now that the sun was up and shining brightly, the woods didn't look creepy the way they had the night before. They were just plain old harmless woods. Turning, Obi spotted the old, gnarled tree that the owl lived in. Obi remembered that when she was in the owl's home, she had heard the German shepherd barking off in the distance.

"We go this way," said Obi, pointing a paw in the direction that she had heard the barking. She knew that once she got to the house where the German shepherd lived, she'd have no trouble finding the way back to the Armstrongs' house.

To Obi's surprise, Kenobi took off in the opposite direction. He dashed over to a log and grabbed something in his mouth.

It was a rubber ball.

"Where did you get that ball?" asked Obi.

"Nowhaaarrr!" Kenobi's words came out all garbled on account of the rubber ball in his mouth.

"You took it from that German shepherd, didn't you?"

Kenobi shook his head. "Naaaawww!"

Obi placed her front paws on her hips. Fixing a stern gaze on the puppy, she said, "Tell the truth, Kenobi."

"Well . . . maybeeee!"

"We have to return it to him."

The puppy's face fell. "Whhhhyyyy?"

"Because it's his, that's why!"

"Pweeese can't I keeeeep eeeet? Pweeese? Pweeese? Pweeese?" begged Kenobi. He gave Obi his cutest sad-eyed puppy dog look.

"Don't give me that look!" cried Obi, feeling a tug in her heart. "Stop it, Kenobi!"

But the puppy didn't stop it. In fact, he did his darnedest to look even cuter. He dropped his ears and made his eyes look bigger, moister, more irresistibly cute.

"Stop it, Kenobi! Stop it this instant!" cried the gerbil. She placed her front paws over her eyes so she wouldn't be tempted to look into the puppy's face.

"Ohhh, aaawww wiiiight! I'll wwwivet wwaack!"

Looking very dejected, Kenobi dropped the rubber ball at Obi's feet. Obi picked up the ball in her two front paws. Having been in Kenobi's mouth, the ball was all wet and slimy.

The two animals headed in the direction of the house where the German shepherd had been barking. Kenobi was so eager to go home and see Rachel again, he kept speeding ahead of Obi and then racing back.

"C'mon, Obi!" he barked impatiently. "Hurry up! Hurry up! You're taking forever!"

"That's because I'm carrying this rubber ball," replied Obi. "Plus, don't forget, I'm a little gerbil. You have bigger legs than me. Tell you what we can do, though. You can carry me."

And so that was what they did. Kenobi dropped to the ground and Obi climbed up onto his back. She took a position at the back of Kenobi's furry neck. Holding the rubber ball under one front paw, Obi grabbed hold of Kenobi's collar with the other.

"Ready when you are!" cried Obi.

With a lurch that almost sent Obi toppling, the puppy sprang to his feet and off they went. Taking huge, leaping bounds, Kenobi dashed through the woods. It was all Obi could do to hold onto his collar and the rubber ball at the same time. Before long they arrived at the edge of the woods, behind the brown house where the really mean German shepherd lived.

Obi glanced about for him. He was nowhere in sight.

"We're in luck!" said Obi. "The really mean dog who lives here must be in his house."

"He's scared of the woods, you know," said Kenobi.

"How do you know that?" asked Obi.

"He never comes into them. Whenever he heard me in the woods, he always stopped right before he got to them."

Now that Kenobi mentioned it, Obi realized that this was exactly what had happened when the German shepherd chased after her, too.

"That is odd," said Obi. "But no time to think about that now. We've got places to go, people to see. Well, a place to go and a girl to see. I'm going to throw the rubber ball into the backyard, and then you and I will continue on our way home."

Clutching the rubber ball in both front paws, Obi climbed up onto the puppy's head. She stood and lifted the ball above her head. Leaning back, Obi gave the ball a good heave into the backyard. The ball flew through the air and landed, bouncing, onto the grass.

Then Kenobi did a very unexpected thing. He leaped forward and bounded into the backyard. Apparently, he thought Obi had thrown the rubber ball for him to chase after!

"Hey!" cried Obi as she lost her balance, fell backward, and began rolling down the back of Kenobi's furry neck.

Chapter Twenty-three

A Big Favor

Just as she was about to go tumbling down the puppy's back, Obi was able to grab Kenobi's leather dog collar. Clutching it tightly with both front paws, Obi held on to the dog collar for dear life.

"Kenobi! What are you doing!?" Obi screamed. "You're not supposed to chase after the ball!"

"I can't help it!" replied Kenobi. "If you throw a ball, I have to fetch it!"

Kenobi raced across the lawn to the ball and snatched it up in his mouth. Suddenly the puppy came to an abrupt stop. Obi felt Kenobi's whole body stiffen. She heard the rubber ball bounce on the lawn, as it dropped out of Kenobi's mouth. Then she heard a growl, a low, vicious, menacing growl.

Obi quickly scrambled up to the top of the puppy's head. She froze. The German shepherd was standing, snarling, in an attack stance in front of Kenobi. He had a fiery, furious look in his eyes.

"Well, well, well!" he said, fixing his glowering eyes upon Obi. "Look who's back! And you told me you weren't a doggy-toy stealer!"

"But I'm not!" protested Obi. "We're here to *return* your favorite rubber ball!"

"Oh, is *that* what you're doing?" replied the German shepherd. He sounded very skeptical. "But hold on a minute! If you're *returning* it, that means you must've *stolen* it!"

"Actually, I prefer to use the word 'borrow,'" said Obi, thinking quickly.

The dog's eyes narrowed at Obi, and he began to growl. Quickly, Obi added, "But if you want to use the word 'stolen,' that's fine with me! Anyway, Kenobi is very sorry that he took your doggy toy without asking. Aren't you, Kenobi?"

The puppy was so terrified, he couldn't speak. All he could do was tremble and whimper.

Obi tried to think of what she could possibly do to mollify the German shepherd. She pointed down at Kenobi and said, "He didn't know it was your ball."

"Correct me if I'm wrong," said the German shepherd,

"but the sign clearly states: 'Beware of Dog! No Stealing Any of His Doggy Toys!'"

"What sign?" asked Obi, puzzled, glancing about the lawn.

"*That* sign!" said the German shepherd. He gestured to a spot behind Obi.

Obi turned to look. Indeed, there was a small sign. Somehow, she had missed it. Which really wasn't surprising, since she had been so focused on keeping an eye on the German shepherd. The sign was on a short metal stake stuck into the lawn, near where the German shepherd's back lawn ended and the next door neighbors' back lawn began.

"And if you happen to miss that sign, there are others posted around the edge of my property," said the German shepherd. "And the warning is on both sides of each sign!"

Obi read the words that were on the sign, but they weren't the words that the German shepherd had said. They weren't even close!

"That's not what that sign says!" said Obi.

"Like you would know!" scoffed the German shepherd.

"As a matter of fact, I would!" replied Obi, insulted. "I can read, you know! The sign says 'Invisible Fence'!"

The dog's face fell. He stared at Obi. He looked incredulous. "Are you sure about that?" he asked.

"Yes, I'm sure!"

"Oh, man!" cried the German shepherd. All at once, he let down his guard. He slumped, and no longer looked so fierce. "That explains everything!"

"It does?" said Obi, surprised.

"Yeah, it does!" groaned the German shepherd. "My owners put up a fence that nobody can see, not even me! This invisible fence stops me from leaving the property— but *only* me! All other creatures can come and go as they please, but not *me!* No! I'm stuck here! I can't leave the property! That's why when I hear strange noises in the woods, I can't go check out who's making them. As soon as I get to the invisible fence, I have to stop! All I can do is bark!"

"Oh! Well, that explains that!" said Obi. It also explained why, the night before, the German shepherd had not chased her into the woods.

"I can't believe my owners would do such a thing!" grumbled the German shepherd.

"Well, sorry I had to be the one to break the news to you," said Obi.

The dog peered at Obi. "So you can read, huh?"

"A little," replied Obi with a modest shrug.

"Since you can read, how would you like to do me a big favor?"

"Like what kind of a big favor?" asked Obi warily.

"I need you to read what it says on the bag of dog food that my owners feed me."

"Why do you want me to do that?"

"Well, to be honest, I'm not sure I can trust my owners anymore," said the German shepherd. "If they put up an invisible fence around the house, who knows what they're feeding me. So what do you say? Will you read it?"

It occurred to Obi that perhaps she could use this favor to her advantage. "If I read it," she said, "will you do *us* a favor? Will you let the two of us go?"

"Yeah, sure, fine, whatever!" replied the German shepherd, with a dismissive wave of his front paw.

From the way the dog had said "Yeah, sure, fine, whatever!" Obi got the distinct impression she could have asked the German shepherd for a much bigger favor.

The German shepherd led the way over to a slate patio where there was a sliding glass door in the rear of the house. The two dogs and Obi—who was still atop

Kenobi's head—gathered in front of the sliding glass door and peered in.

"There, see it?" said the German shepherd, pointing his paw.

Inside Obi spotted a big bag of dog food on the floor.

"Yes, I see the bag," she reported.

"So? What does it say?"

"It says 'Real Beef Flavor.'"

"That is *such* a joke!" cried the German shepherd. "It's not real beef flavor! That dog food hardly has any flavor at all!"

"Well, that's what the bag says," said Obi, shrugging. "Now, if you don't mind, Kenobi and I need to be on our way."

"Well, thanks for bringing this to my attention," said the German shepherd.

"I'm happy I could be of help," replied Obi.

The German shepherd escorted Obi and Kenobi across the back lawn. Suddenly, something on the grass caught Kenobi's attention. He stopped and turned, his eyes cast downward. It was the rub-  ber ball. It was still lying on the grass where Kenobi had dropped it. The German shepherd saw Kenobi eyeing his favorite doggy toy and let out a low growl. That did the trick. Kenobi continued across the lawn. In fact, his step quickened.

When they got to the edge of the dog's property, the German shepherd abruptly stopped. "I'd accompany you farther," he said, "but as you and I both now know, I can't."

"I totally understand," said Obi, and gave the dog a sympathetic hey-don't-give-it-another-thought look. Then, just as Obi was about to say goodbye to the German shepherd, Kenobi broke into a furious run. Caught unawares, Obi lost her balance and somersaulted down the back of the puppy's neck. Once again she managed to grab hold of Kenobi's collar just as she was about to tumble down Kenobi's back. She peered ahead to see what had caused the puppy to bolt.

She should have guessed. Kenobi had spotted a gray house in the distance.

It was the Armstrongs' house, his home.

Her home.

Their home!

Chapter Twenty-four

Trapped!

Obi knew the puppy could run fast, but she had no idea just how fast until they were on their way home, with the Armstrongs' gray house in sight.

Like the puppy, Obi could not wait to see Rachel again. She couldn't wait to see Rachel's face when she saw Obi riding on top of the puppy, standing on her hind legs and holding on to Kenobi's collar, like a gladiator boldly astride a blazing, golden chariot. The girl was bound to put two and two together and come to the conclusion that Obi had found the puppy and brought him home. Rachel would be so happy to see Kenobi, but, Obi hoped, she would be even happier to see the gerbil, her puppy rescuer.

Kenobi dashed into the Armstrongs' backyard.

He was bounding across the lawn when, over by the

shrubs that grew alongside the Armstrongs' house, Obi heard frantic thrashing sounds.

"Help! Help!" a terrified voice shouted from within the bushes. "Someone, please, help me! I'm not a criminal! Honest, I'm not!"

No, it couldn't be, thought Obi.

"I don't want to end up like my Uncle Leroy! Really, I don't! Help! Someone, please, help me!"

It was *him,* all right. It was that daffy squirrel!

"Kenobi, wait!" cried Obi.

"I can't wait!" replied Kenobi. "I want to go see Rachel."

"I want to see her, too!" said Obi. "But hear all that yelling? Someone needs our help! And I think I know who!"

Kenobi showed no interest in either finding out who it could be or in helping. The puppy continued straight to the Armstrongs' kitchen screen door. So Obi took matters into her own paws. She grasped Kenobi's dog collar tightly in her front paws and threw her weight in the direction of the bushes. This caused the puppy to veer in that direction.

Now, if it had been just Obi investigating the situation, she would have approached the scene very cautiously, creeping into the bushes, glancing warily about. But that was not Kenobi's style. The puppy's style was to crash through the shrubs.

The squirrel was caught in a rectangular trap that was made of heavy gauge wire, beside the cement foundation of the house. The trap had two metal doors at each end. The doors had closed on the squirrel, so he couldn't escape. The squirrel looked absolutely terrified. He was freaking out, doing flips and slamming his body against the sides of the cage.

And that was *before* he saw Kenobi. When the squirrel glimpsed the dog, he screamed, "Oh, no! First a trap! Now a dog! I can't deal with this!"

Obi scrambled to the top of Kenobi's head so the squirrel would see her.

"Calm down, Squirrel!" cried Obi. "It's me, Obi!"

The squirrel stopped and stared up at Obi. "Obi?" he said, surprised.

"Yes, it's me! You don't have to worry about this dog. Remember that puppy I said I was looking for? Well, this is him. He's a good dog. What are you doing in that cage?"

"I was trying to help *you*!" wailed the squirrel.

"Me?"

"You told me to go get help!"

"*I* did?"

"When that owl flew off with you, you yelled, "Quick, Squirrel, go get help!""

Now Obi remembered. She couldn't imagine who the squirrel would be getting help from. "Who were you getting help from?"

"Mr. Durkins, of course!" replied the squirrel. "You know, your little mouse pal who lives in the Armstrongs' house."

"How did you end up in this cage?" Obi asked.

"I was running around the outside of the house, looking for Mr. Durkins, when I came upon this cage. It had a small pile of nuts in it! Well, you know me! I love nuts! So I thought I'd try one. I went into the cage, and then suddenly—*bam!*—the two doors crashed down, trapping me inside. Look at me, Obi! I'm a criminal, like you, trapped in a cage! I don't want to be a criminal! I don't want to end up like my Uncle Leroy! He got caught in a cage just like this, and nobody has seen or heard from him since!"

The squirrel burst into tears.

"It's okay, Squirrel," said Obi. She felt bad for the creature—and guilty. If she hadn't told the squirrel to go get help, he wouldn't be trapped in this cage. Obi had told the squirrel she looked out for her friends, that she wouldn't let bad things happen to them. Well, here he was, stuck in a trap, the thing the squirrel feared most. "Don't you worry, Squirrel!" Obi went on. "We're going to get you out of there!"

"How?" blubbered the squirrel. "I've been trying to get out of this cage since last night. It's escape-proof!"

"There's *got* to be a way," said Obi. She put a paw on her chin and studied the cage. The squirrel had said that the cage doors had crashed down after he entered the cage. Obi wondered what would happen if she were to pull up on one of the doors.

Obi decided to give it a try. She had Kenobi move closer to the cage. Then she jumped down from the puppy's head to the top of the cage. She stepped over to one of the doors. Using both front paws, Obi pulled up. The cage door began to lift! Before Obi could lift it any higher, though, Kenobi started sniffing the cage, which caused the squirrel to have another panic attack. He went berserk, slamming his body against the sides of the cage. Obi toppled over, letting go of the cage door. The cage door crashed down.

Obi sprang to her feet. "Squirrel!" she cried. "You need to stop bouncing around! I can't open the door with you bouncing around like that!"

But the squirrel was so distressed, running around the inside of the cage, Obi wasn't even sure he had heard her. Obi had to get the squirrel to stay still. But how? Then Obi thought of something. Well, actually, someone.

Obi focused her gaze on the puppy and said, "Kenobi, I need you to bring me over to the Armstrongs' woodpile."

"Why?" Clearly, this was not something Kenobi wanted to do. All he wanted to do was run to the kitchen screen door and let Rachel know he was back home.

Obi knew the puppy didn't have the attention span for a long explanation, so she simply replied, "I just do!"

"Oh, all right! But then can we go see Rachel?"

"Yes, absolutely!" replied Obi.

Obi hopped back onto the puppy's back, and Kenobi raced over to the woodpile that was at the edge of the woods.

"Gertrude!" Obi shouted at the woodpile. "It's me, Obi! I need your help!"

Obi saw Gertrude's small, plump figure inside the dark log cave. Using her cane to walk, Gertrude limped out into the open air. "Obi, you're back!" Her eyes widened at the sight of Kenobi. She pointed her cane at him and said, "Who's this?"

"This is Kenobi," replied Obi. "This is the puppy I was looking for."

"You found him!" exclaimed Gertrude. "Good for you! I told you you would find him!"

"Look, Gertrude, I need your help. Can you come with us for a moment?"

"You want *me* to ride on top of that dog?" Gertrude did not sound too thrilled about the idea.

"If you don't mind, yes," said Obi. "Don't worry—you'll be safe. Really."

Gertrude turned to the mouth of the cave. She yelled to the mice who were inside the cave to continue drawing, that she'd be right back. "Okay," she said to Obi. She trusted Obi so much that she showed no hesitation as she stepped onto the puppy's back.

Once Gertrude was safely on board, Kenobi raced back to the caged squirrel. The squirrel was still flipping out, crashing against the wire walls of his prison.

"Oh, my!" gasped Gertrude.

"I need you to get this squirrel to stop moving," said Obi.

"I think I can do that," replied Gertrude.

"I *know* you can do that!" said Obi with a smile.

Both at once, Obi and Gertrude slid off Kenobi's back and onto the top of the cage. From there, Gertrude climbed down to the ground. Obi took her position at one of the cage doors. She looked down at Gertrude and said, "Ready when you are!"

With a stern look on her face, Gertrude glared at the squirrel and bellowed:

"DON'T MOVE!"

The squirrel instantly froze. He did not move a muscle. The only thing that moved on the squirrel were his eyes: they followed Gertrude.

Obi quickly went to work. She gave the door a good yank up. The door lifted. She gave it another yank. The door slid up higher. Obi yanked and yanked again. The door rose higher and higher. When Obi didn't think she could yank any higher, she yelled down to Gertrude, "Okay!"

"MOVE IT!" shouted Gertrude.

The squirrel bolted. He scampered out through the narrow opening under the cage door. As soon as the squirrel was

free again, Obi let go of the door. It fell with a crash.

The squirrel hurried over to a bush, stopped, and spun about. Peering up at Obi on top of the cage, he said, "I'm sorry, Obi, but I can't do this anymore! I can't be part of your gang! The life of a criminal is just too stressful for me!"

And before Obi had a chance to respond, the squirrel scurried out across the Armstrongs' back lawn toward his maple tree. The last Obi saw of the squirrel was his fluffy gray tail twitching nervously in the air as he scampered up the trunk of the tree.

Obi leaped off the cage and landed beside Gertrude. "Thanks, Gertrude," she said. "I couldn't have done it without you."

"Glad I could be of help," said the mouse.

"I'll get Kenobi to give you a lift back to the—" Obi started to say when, glancing about, she stopped.

The puppy was gone!

"Oh, no!" groaned Obi. She had a pretty good idea where Kenobi had disappeared to. Obi turned to Gertrude and said, "I'm sorry, Gertrude, I guess I can't offer you a lift back to your woodpile, after all."

"No worries," said Gertrude. "I know the way."

The mouse and the gerbil said goodbye to each other,

hugged, and then Gertrude headed out across the Armstrongs' back lawn toward her woodpile.

Obi swung around and quickly made her way behind the shrubs to the side of the house, where the kitchen door was located. She hoped she wasn't too late. Her heart was thumping as she came around the corner of the house. She saw the kitchen screen door, and froze.

Kenobi was standing outside the screen door, wagging his tail, scratching his front paws on the screen part of the door.

"Kenobi?!" Obi heard a very startled girl's voice cry out from inside the kitchen.

It was Rachel. The screen door burst open, and Obi saw Rachel come out of the house. "You're back!" she cried happily as she bent down and picked up the puppy.

By now, Kenobi's tail was wagging so fast, it was amazing it didn't break off and fly into the air. The puppy barked a couple of thrilled barks to let Rachel know that yes, yes, it was him!

"Mom! Dad! Look who's back!" shouted Rachel, her voice bubbling with excitement and joy. She cuddled the puppy in her arms and brought Kenobi back into the house. The screen door slapped closed behind them.

For a long, heartbreaking moment, Obi just stood

there, stunned, staring at the screen door. She could not believe what had just happened. Rachel had been reunited with Kenobi, her lost puppy, which was a good thing, but it would have been a much better thing if Obi could have been with Kenobi, too.

A tear slid down Obi's furry face. She felt a lump in her throat and, for a moment, it was all Obi could do to keep from bursting into sobs. How would Rachel ever know now that Obi, her brave Jedi gerbil knight, had ventured outdoors into the dangerous world, found the little puppy, and brought him back home.

She wouldn't!

Chapter Twenty-five Look Who's Back!

With tears in her eyes, Obi trudged to the back of the Armstrongs' house. She felt utterly desolate as she made her way behind the shrubs. It pained her to think that things would go back to the way they had been, with Kenobi getting all of Rachel's love and attention, and Obi getting whatever crumbs of the girl's affection that remained. Just thinking about it made Obi's eyes fill up with a new round of tears.

Rather than return to her cage by way of the kitchen screen door, Obi had decided to take the secret passageway back. Now that Kenobi and Rachel had been reunited, what was the point of entering the house through the screen door?

There was none. Besides, Obi was so small she couldn't scratch the screen the way Kenobi could and let someone know she was there. She would have to wait outside the kitchen door until one of the Armstrongs left the house, and who knew how long *that* would be?

The little entrance to the secret passageway was in the rear of the Armstrongs' house, on the wall behind the coiled-up green garden hose. Obi was heading for it when she heard a strange sound. She stopped to listen. It was a jangling sound, the kind of sound a little bell makes. It came from behind one of the rhododendron bushes. Just then, who should step out from the bush, jingling as she did, but the black-and-white cat, Sweetie Smoochkins! She had a little bell that dangled from her collar, just below her chin.

"Well, well! Look who's back!" said Sweetie Smoochkins. Her voice did not sound exactly thrilled to see the little gerbil. "Where have *you* been, Fuzzball?"

"Oh . . . nowhere really," replied Obi with a shrug. She didn't feel much like talking about it. "What's with the bell?" she asked, changing the subject.

"Do you like it?" asked Sweetie Smoochkins.

To be perfectly honest, Obi thought it was a rather hideous fashion accessory. Who would want to listen to a jingling bell all the time? Everywhere you went, it would jingle. But Obi was too kind to say such a thing.

If Sweetie Smoochkins wanted to wear a little bell that jingled, well, that was her choice.

"It's nice," said Obi.

"I'm glad *you* like it, Fuzzball," replied Sweetie Smoochkins. "Because *I* hate it!"

Obi was surprised. "You do? Then why are you wearing it?"

"Because of *you!*"

Obi was even more surprised. *"Me?!"*

The cat's eyes narrowed to practically slits. "Yes, *you!* All three of us cats have to wear bells now thanks to *you!*"

"What did *I* do?"

"You disappeared!"

Obi could not understand how that would cause the cats to have to wear bells on their collars. Was she missing something? "Am I missing something?" she asked.

"When you disappeared, Rachel was absolutely devastated," said the cat.

Obi blinked in surprise. "She—she was?!"

"Yes, she was!" said Sweetie Smoochkins. "Oh, sure, she was upset when that drippy puppy disappeared, but you, well, *you* broke her heart when you vanished!"

Obi was astounded. "I . . . I did?"

"At first, Rachel thought the twins had taken you out of your cage. But when you didn't turn up, we three cats got blamed. The Armstrongs leaped to the conclusion that it was one of us who caused you to mysteriously disappear."

Obi could see how the Armstrongs might come to that conclusion. Obi decided to keep this thought to herself, though. All she said was "But you had nothing to do with my disappearance."

"Of course I didn't!" said Sweetie Smoochkins. "Nor did Honey Buns or Sugar Smacks! But none of the Armstrongs know that! So now we each have to wear a bell so little, unsuspecting creatures like you will be warned that we might be sneaking up."

"Well, don't worry!" said Obi. "I'm on my way back to my cage now. The Armstrongs will find out soon enough that I'm safe and sound."

"Oh, but will they?" asked Sweetie Smoochkins.

Obi did not like the way the cat said this. It sounded very cryptic. "What does that mean?"

"Think about it, Fuzzball," said Sweetie Smoochkins. "Here you are, outside in the shrubs, and here I am, outside in the shrubs, and, well, I'm a cat and you're a gerbil and cats eat gerbils and this would be a perfect place to eat you, since none of the Armstrongs would ever know."

"Oh!" said Obi, who really wasn't thinking along these lines. "But if you eat me, Sweetie Smoochkins, the Armstrongs will never know that you had nothing to do with my disappearance. You'll have to keep wearing that bell on your collar!"

Sweetie Smoochkins lifted her two front paws and pretended she was weighing two invisible objects. She moved one paw up and down at the same time she moved the other paw up and down. It looked as if she was trying to make up her mind which invisible object weighed more. "Let's see . . ." said the cat. "Having to wear a bell or getting to eat a gerbil. Such a hard choice! *Hmm!* I think I'll go with eating the gerbil! I haven't had a good gerbil in ages! In fact, I don't think I've *ever* had a gerbil!"

Had this been any other time, Obi would have been nervous as anything and her heart would have been banging inside her chest, she would have been so scared. Yet, oddly enough, she wasn't afraid—not in the least. That was because Sweetie Smoochkins had made a mistake— a rather colossal mistake. She had said that Obi had broken Rachel's heart by disappearing. Well, *that* was all Obi needed to hear! The little gerbil was now bound and determined to be reunited with Rachel! Nothing was going to stop her from completing her mission—not even Sweetie Smoochkins!

As Obi tried to think of how she could get past Sweetie Smoochkins and disappear into the secret passageway, she heard the jingle of another little bell. It came from behind her. Then she heard a startled voice say, "For crying out loud! Look who's back!"

Obi swung around and saw Honey Buns, the honey-colored cat, emerge from behind a rhododendron bush. The cat's eyes were wide with astonishment at seeing Obi.

"Hawo, Honey Buns!" said Obi.

"Where have *you* been?" asked Honey Buns. "You know, the Armstrongs all think you're dead!"

"Who's dead?" asked another voice. Obi heard yet another tingling bell as the tiger cat, Sugar Smacks, popped out from behind another rhododendron bush. Sugar Smacks stopped in her tracks and stared at the gerbil.

"Obi?!"

"Hawo, Sugar Smacks!"

"Where the heck have you been?" demanded Sugar Smacks. "Do you know how much trouble you've gotten us cats into?"

"Yeah, I know and I'm really sorry about that," said Obi.

"Oh, I bet you are!" said Sweetie Smoochkins.

All this time, Obi had been wondering how on earth she was ever going to get back to her cage. As if things weren't complicated enough, the three cats had all encircled her. Worse, their tails had all begun to do that awful swirling and swishing thing they always did whenever they were around Obi. It was a good thing the cats had been so confused to see Obi again—otherwise one of them surely would have attacked the little gerbil by now.

Wait! What if Obi were to confuse the cats even more? If she got them really confused, she might just be able to sneak away.

Well, it was worth a try.

"It's all Honey Buns's fault!" Obi blurted out, pointing an accusatory paw at Honey Buns.

Honey Buns frowned at Obi. "*My* fault?! What are you talking about?"

"You wanted me to hide so Sweetie Smoochkins and Sugar Smacks would get into trouble!"

"*What!?*" cried Honey Buns.

Obi turned to Sweetie Smoochkins. "That was what you told me to say, right?"

Honey Buns fixed her eyes on Sweetie Smoochkins. "What is she talking about?"

"I haven't a clue!" replied Sweetie Smoochkins.

"Oh, like I'm supposed to believe that?" said Honey Buns.

"But I don't!" insisted Sweetie Smoochkins.

Obi turned and winked at Sugar Smacks. "It's working!" she whispered.

Honey Buns and Sweetie Smoochkins both glowered at Sugar Smacks.

"I saw that wink!" cried Honey Buns.

"What's working?" demanded Sweetie Smoochkins.

"I don't know!" replied the tiger cat, looking totally befuddled.

"Uh-oh!" said Obi. "This isn't working out the way you thought it would, is it, Honey Buns?"

Sugar Smacks hissed at Honey Buns. "How did you think it was going to work out, Honey Buns?" she asked.

Honey Buns hissed right back at Sugar Smacks. "Don't you dare hiss at me like that!" she warned. By now, Sweetie Smoochkins was so riled up that she, too, hissed at Sugar Smacks.

The cats broke into a quarrel. It quickly escalated

into a big catfight, with lots of loud hissing and accusations. Obi, still facing the cats, quietly stepped back from the fight, without any of them noticing. She glanced up at the coiled garden hose. The end of the hose was dangling about six inches from 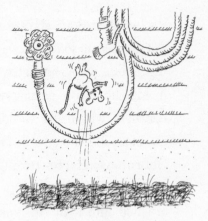 where Obi stood. Obi waited for a particularly heated moment between the cats, and then, when none of them was paying attention to her, she leaped up and grabbed hold of the garden hose with her two front paws. She pulled herself up and scampered up the hose to the hidden entrance of the secret passageway, then slipped into the tunnel without being seen by the cats.

Inside the dark tunnel, Obi heard Sugar Smacks cry out, "Hey, where did Obi go?"

"She was here just a second ago!" said Honey Buns.

"You idiots!" cried Sweetie Smoochkins. "Don't you see what that gerbil just did? She tricked us! Well, it doesn't matter. I've got a feeling that when Fuzzball finds out what's in store for her when she gets back to

Rachel's bedroom, she's going to wish we *had* eaten her!"

Obi had no idea what Sweetie Smoochkins was talking about. Nor, honestly, did she care. She was safe inside the secret passageway, heading back to Rachel's bedroom, where she would be reunited with her adoptive mother. The thought of being with Rachel again made Obi run even faster through the dark tunnel.

And then—*bam!*—Obi slammed into a wall. She crashed into it at full speed! Obi bounced off the wall and fell backward onto her bum-bum. She sat on the dusty floor of the secret passageway, dazed, staring at the black smudge in front of her, wondering who on earth had put a wall up in the secret passage. Obi sprang to her feet and began banging her front paws against the wall.

"Open up!" she cried.

Obi stopped banging her fists against the wall and took a step back. She was all ready to slam her shoulder against the wall to try and bust through when she remembered something. When Mr. Durkins was taking her through the secret passageway to the outside world, they had passed through a secret panel. *This* must be that secret panel! Obi tried to remember how Mr. Durkins had opened the panel. Unfortunately, the light had been so dim, she had been unable to see. Obi began groping the wall, feeling around for a secret button or something that might open the door. She felt nothing, though. Then she tried sliding the door, the way a human would push open a sliding glass door.

It worked! The secret panel slid open!

Obi was about to break into a run again when she had the most terrible fright. Up ahead in the darkness, positioned right smack in the middle of the secret passageway, stood a small, stooped figure. Obi stopped in her tracks. She screamed.

"Aaaaaahhhh!"

The figure moved toward her and into the thin light. It was the old mouse, Mr. Durkins.

"Mr. Durkins!" cried Obi, placing a paw over her furiously beating heart. "You scared the daylights out of me!"

"You're back!" said Mr. Durkins.

It was such a typical Mr. Durkins greeting. No "Hawo!" No "Sorry to startle you, Obi!" Nope, just a curt "You're back!"

"Yes, I'm back!" replied Obi as she quickly squeezed

past the old mouse. "Sorry, Mr. Durkins, but I can't talk now! I need to get back to my cage!" She began to run again.

"Kid, wait!" cried Mr. Durkins, hobbling urgently after her. "I need to tell you something! It's important!"

"I know what you're going to say!" replied Obi, glancing over her shoulder at the old mouse. "The Armstrongs think I'm dead!"

"No, it's not that!"

"Then it must be the cats!" said Obi. "I know all about them, too, and the little bells they have to wear now on account of me. I know they're all really angry at me. Don't worry, Mr. Durkins. I'll be careful!"

Mr. Durkins yelled out something, but Obi was scurrying so fast through the dark tunnel, she was unable to hear what he said.

Obi followed the secret passageway as it sloped up to the second floor. Because it was so dark and hard to see in the secret passageway, Obi had a tendency when she was rushing through it to overshoot her mark and miss the little hole that led out into Rachel's bedroom. Not this time, though! Obi made sure she didn't run past the little hole!

Rachel wasn't in her bedroom. Obi stepped out of the hole and raced across the yellow shag carpet to Rachel's dresser. She ran to the side of the dresser and grabbed hold of the lamp cord that dangled over the side. She climbed up the cord in record time and hurried across the dresser to her cage.

Just as Obi was about to climb back into her cage, she saw, to her astonishment, that the little square cage door was closed. How could it be closed? Obi was positive she had left it slightly ajar. Then Obi realized that Rachel must have closed the cage door. She had probably closed it after turning the cage inside out, searching for Obi.

Obi tried to pull the cage door open with her front paws, but she couldn't get a good grip on the bars. Then an idea occurred to her. She wrapped the end of her tail around one of the bars of the cage and pulled. The door sprang open. Obi hopped into her cage, closing the cage door behind her with her tail.

Out in the bedroom hallway, Obi heard footsteps coming up the stairs. They were Rachel's footsteps! Obi's heart felt like it was about to explode, it was beating so fast. Excited as anything, Obi waited for Rachel to appear in the bedroom doorway.

It was then that Obi saw it—the computer on Rachel's desk. The screen on the computer showed a photo of Obi and Rachel!

Obi couldn't take her eyes off the computer screen. Rachel had chosen her, not Kenobi, for her computer screen saver!

Obi felt so happy, so honored, so loved!

At that moment, Rachel walked into room, with a very squirming Kenobi in her arms. A few days ago, Obi would have been terribly jealous to see Kenobi in Rachel's arms, but not now, not after finding out how much she had been missed and after seeing this photo of herself on Rachel's computer screen.

Obi rose onto her hind legs so Rachel would see her. But the girl was so focused on Kenobi she didn't notice Obi. But then why would Rachel glance over at Obi's cage? As far as the girl was concerned, Obi was gone. Well, Obi would just have to fix that misconception, wouldn't she? She hopped onto her squeaky exercise wheel and began to run. No, not just run—fly!

Squeak! Squeak! Squeak! Squeak!

Rachel, hearing the squeaks, looked over. Her eyes widened in disbelief and her mouth dropped open.

"*Obi?!* Is . . . is that y*ou*? Oh, my gosh! It *is* you!"

She dropped Kenobi unceremoniously onto the floor and hurried over to Obi's cage. The moment Kenobi's paws touched the bedroom carpet, he spun about and beat it out of Rachel's bedroom, disappearing into the bedroom hallway.

Obi hopped off her exercise wheel and hurried over to the front of her cage so she could greet her adoptive mother.

"Hawo, Mom! I'm back!" cried Obi as stood up on her hind legs.

Rachel flung open the cage door, picked Obi up in her hand, and took the gerbil out of her cage.

"Obi!" exclaimed Rachel, gently stroking a finger on top of the little gerbil's head. "Where did you go? I am so glad you're back! I missed you *so* much!"

"I missed you *so* much, too, Mom!" Obi tried to say through the tender look in her eyes.

"It's so weird that you and Kenobi both came back on the same day," said Rachel. "The *same* morning!" Her eyes studied Obi closely as she said, "Did you have something to do with that?"

Obi shrugged and gave her adoptive mother a "well . . . maybe" look.

Rachel leaned close to Obi and whispered, "Don't tell

Kenobi or Wan, but you'll always hold a special place in my heart, Obi."

Obi thought her heart was going to burst with happiness. Telling a pet you hold a special place in your heart probably isn't something that's recommended in pet training manuals, but Obi didn't care. Of course, Obi would never tell Kenobi or Wan. And then Obi's joy turned to bewilderment. Wan? Who was *Wan*?

Just then, out in the bedroom hallway, Obi heard a curious *clunk!* sound. Then she heard another curious *clunk!* If Obi hadn't known any better, she would have sworn it sounded like a Gerbil Mobile banging up against a wall by someone who couldn't navigate it very well.

Rachel heard the clunks, too. She glanced toward her bedroom doorway, then quickly back at Obi. "Obi," she said. "There's something I need to tell you."

But before Rachel could say another word, something in the doorway caught Obi's eye, down by the floor. Something had rolled into the bedroom. Obi stared in shock. It was a Gerbil Mobile. No, not *a* Gerbil Mobile, *Obi's* Gerbil Mobile!

Obi, aghast, could not believe what she saw. A little gerbil was inside her Gerbil Mobile! The clear plastic ball was being pushed by a perfectly delighted Kenobi. The puppy swatted the Gerbil Mobile with his front paws, like it was a beach ball.

"Mom! Mom!" cried the young gerbil excitedly as the Gerbil Mobile rolled across the bedroom carpet. "Look at me! Look at me!"

Obi lifted her gaze and met her adoptive mother's eyes. The two of them looked at each other for a moment. Then, together, they turned their heads and stared at the little gerbil that was running and bouncing about inside the Gerbil Mobile.

"Obi," said Rachel, "I'd like you to meet Wan."

Turn the page for a preview of the
next book about Obi . . .

Gerbil ON A
School Trip!

It was all Mr. Durkins's fault! It was all because of him that Wan was chewing on the bars of his cage again!

Wan was not chewing on his bars because his little gerbil teeth were coming in and he needed something to gnaw on. *That*, Obi felt, would be understandable! Annoying, yes, but understandable!

Nor was he doing it to get Rachel's attention. That, too, would be understandable. After all, Obi herself sometimes gnawed on the bars of her cage to get Rachel to glance over. As soon as she did, Obi would stop gnawing instantly.

No, Wan was chewing on the bars of his cage for no other reason than to get on Rachel's nerves!

Rachel was at her desk on the other side of the bedroom, trying to do her homework. Pencil in hand, a look of deep concentration on her face, Rachel leaned over her desk and wrote in her spiral-bound notebook. Wan, meanwhile, was in his cage, gnawing away, being as annoying as anything, trying des-  perately to shatter that look of deep concentration on Rachel's face.

It was all because of Mr. Durkins that Wan was being so annoying. Mr. Durkins was the old, bitter mouse who lived up in the Armstrongs' attic. He hated the Armstrongs! He loathed every single one of them, even—if you can believe it—Obi's dear, sweet adoptive mother! Apparently, Mr. Durkins had only one goal in life: to make the Armstrongs' lives absolutely miserable!

He was an evil mouse, Mr. Durkins! His new diabolical plan involved Wan. He had taught the little gerbil how to chew on the bars of his cage and had instructed Wan to do it as often as possible—but only when Rachel was in her bedroom. He knew the noise, grating as it was, would drive Rachel nuts.

And it did!

Wan, who didn't know any better, was only too happy to do whatever Mr. Durkins asked. Wan had become Mr. Durkins's little helper, his protégé. He did everything that nasty, little mouse told him to, no questions asked. Worse, Wan seemed to really enjoy doing as Mr. Durkins instructed. Right now, for instance, he was giggling to himself as he chewed on his bars. It made Wan sound so sinister. Either that, or a gerbil with a serious giggling problem.

Rachel was doing her best to ignore Wan. At one point, she cupped her hands over her ears so as not to hear him. But honestly, how can you write with your hands over your ears? You can't! Finally losing her temper, Rachel flashed a fierce look at Wan and snapped, "Will you stop it, Wan! You're driving me nuts! Can't you see I'm trying to do my homework?"

"Yes, Wan, knock it off, will you!" exclaimed Obi, squeaking in Gerbil. "You're driving *me* nuts, too!"

But did Wan listen to either Rachel or Obi? No! He kept right on gnawing—gnawing and giggling!

The thing was, Obi really wanted Rachel to do a good job on her homework. That afternoon Rachel had come home from school very excited. Tossing her backpack onto the floor of her bedroom, she fixed her eyes on Obi and said, "Guess what, Obi? Guess what my homework assignment for tonight is?"

Obi, who was in her cage, was startled. Since when did Rachel get so excited about homework? As far as Obi could tell, Rachel hated homework! Every evening, it seemed, she complained about how much homework she had to do. A school night didn't go by that Mrs. Armstrong didn't have to stick her head into Rachel's bedroom and ask her if she had done her homework yet. So what was so exciting about today's homework assignment? With a quizzical look on her small whiskered face, Obi peered at Rachel through the bars of her cage.

"I have to write a paper about my favorite pet! You'll never guess *who* that is!"

Obi smiled to herself. Oh, she had a pretty good idea! It was Obi, of course! Who else could it be? It certainly wasn't Wan, not with his incessant gnawing! And Obi was almost certain it wasn't Rachel's other pet, either, the golden retriever puppy, Kenobi. It might've been Kenobi once, back when he was a cute, little, helpless, and hapless puppy. But lately, Kenobi had been growing by leaps and bounds and no longer looked like the cuddliest thing on earth. The puppy was also no longer allowed to hang out up in Rachel's bedroom, the way he used to.

To be fair, this wasn't really Kenobi's fault. Mr. Armstrong had made it a rule that Kenobi, who was quite furry and tended to shed a lot, could no longer be upstairs where all the Armstrongs' bedrooms were located. But still! Had it been Obi, she would have found a way upstairs, rule or no rule! Nothing would ever keep *her* from being with Rachel! That was the kind of pet Obi was!

Obi's cage sat on top of Rachel's dresser, right beside Wan's cage. Obi went over to the side of her cage that faced Wan and glowered at the little gerbil. He was so busy chewing on the bars of his cage—and giggling to himself—he didn't even notice Obi.

"Stop gnawing, Wan!" Obi ordered.

Wan paid no attention.

"Did you hear me, Wan?"

Apparently not: he kept on gnawing and giggling!

"I SAID STOP GNAWING, WAN! STOP IT THIS INSTANT!"

That got Wan to stop! He turned and gave Obi a very bewildered look. "But Mr. D told me to chew on my bars when Rachel is in her bedroom."

Obi frowned. "Mr. D?"

"You know, Mr. Durkins! He told me to call him Mr. D!"

"He did?" Obi couldn't help but feel a little hurt. Mr. Durkins had never asked *her* to call him Mr. D. But then why would he? It wasn't like she and Mr. Durkins were friends. The fact was, Obi disapproved of everything Mr. Durkins did. "When did he ask you to do that?" she inquired.

"One time when you were asleep in your cage."

"Well, Wan," said Obi, "I really don't care what Mr. D—*Mr. Durkins*—told you to do! *I'm* telling you to *stop* gnawing!"

"But Mr. D won't like that!"

"I don't care! Rachel has a very important home-work assignment to do," explained Obi. "She needs you to be very quiet so she can concentrate. Your chewing on your bars is getting on Rachel's nerves!"

"But that's what Mr. D *wants* me to do!"

"Yes, I know but that's not what *I* want you to do!"

"But *you're* not Mr. D!"

Obi tried to stay calm. It wasn't easy! She wanted to wring Wan's little neck. Since that was out of the question, Obi did the next best thing: she glared at Wan. She gave him her most withering stare. Obi was trying to think of what else she could do (since her most withering stare didn't seem to be having much of an effect on Wan) when she heard Rachel chuckle to herself. Obi swung about and saw that Rachel had a smile on her face. The girl was at her desk, pencil in hand, smiling and staring straight ahead, completely lost in thought. Evidently, she had remembered some funny incident she had had with her favorite pet.

Obi smiled, too. She had no idea what happy memory Rachel had recalled, but it had to be something good. Was it that time she and

Rachel went to the gerbil convention together? They sure had a blast that day, didn't they?

All at once, Rachel began writing furiously again. For his part, Wan began gnawing furiously again. After a couple of minutes of intense writing, Rachel tossed her pencil down on the desk and blurted out, "Finished!"

Obi watched as Rachel ripped a sheet of paper out of her spiral-bound notebook. Leaping up from the desk, Rachel went over to her blue backpack, which was on the floor, unzipped it, and stuck in her homework paper.

Chapter Two

Serious Doubts!

That night, just before Rachel's bedtime, Mr. Armstrong came into Rachel's bedroom to say good night and to read her a story aloud. It was a ritual the two of them shared, a special time they had together. He'd been doing it for as long as Obi could remember. Mr. Armstrong and Rachel always sat together in Rachel's comfy blue armchair, in a pool of soft lamplight, while Mr. Armstrong read. The chair was beside Rachel's dresser—which was where Obi's cage sat. Some evenings Mr. Armstrong read a book that could be finished in one sitting. Other times, he read a big book that took several evenings—sometimes even several weeks—to complete. Like tonight's book was *The Subtle Knife*, the second book in the trilogy His Dark Materials.

While Rachel, dressed in her jammies, cuddled up

close beside her father and listened, Obi sat in the bedroom tower of her cage, listening.

Yet, Obi wasn't *just* listening. As she listened, Obi was also peering down at the words on the pages of the book and connecting them to the words that Mr. Armstrong was reading aloud. It was by doing this that Obi, after many, many books, had learned how to read.

Yes, that's right, Obi could read! It was Obi's little secret—something no one else knew about. Well, except Mr. Durkins. He knew Obi could read. But that was only because he made it his business to know everybody else's business in the Armstrongs' house! Oh, and a couple of dogs in the neighborhood also knew Obi could read. (It's a long story, but Obi had told them she could read.) So maybe it wasn't such a big secret, after all.

Mr. Armstrong was at that part of the book in which Lyra and Will, the two main characters, had just entered another world than the one they were in. Will had used a knife, the subtle knife, to slice open a piece of air, which allowed him and Lyra to enter this new world. Obi, fascinated, was anxious to find out more about this other world. But just as Lyra and Will were about to venture into this new world, Mrs. Armstrong came into the room to say good night to Rachel.

Mr. Armstrong stopped reading and said, "Well, I think this is where we'll stop for tonight." And with that, he marked the page with a piece of paper and closed the book! Obi was flabbergasted! How could Mr. Armstrong stop at such a suspenseful part of the story!?

"Oh, can't we read a little more?" begged Rachel.

Which was exactly what Obi was hoping Rachel would say! Obi and her adoptive mother were alike in so many ways. Rachel loved a good bedtime story just as much as Obi did.

"Sorry, kiddo, but it's beddy-bye time," said Mr. Armstrong. "You've got school tomorrow. Someone needs a good night's sleep."

Rachel, who slept on the top bunk of a bunk bed, climbed the ladder up to her bed and slipped under the covers. Mr. Armstrong tucked her in and gave her a good-night kiss on top of her head. As he left the room, he turned off the lights.

Now that the room was dark, Obi nestled down under a big pile of cedar shavings in her bedroom tower. She closed her eyes to go to sleep. But she couldn't sleep. She was too wired. She couldn't stop thinking about the story Mr. Armstrong had read. She kept wondering about this new world that Lyra and Will had entered and what it would be like. It was driving Obi crazy not knowing!

The lights hadn't been off for more than a few minutes when Obi, still wide awake, heard a slow, deep, steady, rhythmic breathing sound coming from the upper bed of the bunk bed—it was the sound Rachel always made when she was asleep. Then Obi heard Wan rustling about in his cage. Then, just like that, the rustling stopped, which meant that Wan, too, had fallen asleep.

Obi tried again to go to sleep. It was no use, though. She was too excited. How Obi wished she could enter a new world.

Suddenly Obi's eyes flung open. She had the eerie sensation that someone was on the dresser outside her cage, lurking in the darkness! Her heart now pounding wildly, Obi peered down from her domed bedroom tower.

She let out a startled gasp. A small dark figure, a shadowy smudge, stood on the dresser between her cage and Wan's.

It was Darth Vadar!

No, wait, that wasn't Darth Vadar! Straining to see in the darkness, Obi now saw it was Mr. Durkins. He was standing up on his hind legs, all hunched over. In the inky darkness, he looked just like Darth Vadar!

Obi slipped down the tube that connected her bedroom tower and the downstairs of her cage. "Mr. Durkins!" she said, speaking to him through the bars of her cage. "What are you doing here?"

"Oh, just looking in on Boy Wonder."

Obi frowned. "Boy Wonder? Who's that?" Then, all at once, she knew. "Oh, no! You're not talking about Wan, are you?"

"I sure am!" replied Mr. Durkins. "I'm so proud of my boy! He did a super good job today!"

"First of all, Mr. Durkins, he's not your boy. And what do you mean he did a super good job? Doing what?"

"Annoying Rachel, of course! Did you see the way he got her to lose her temper? The boy is a natural!"

Obi shook her head in disbelief and dismay. Mr. Durkins may not have been Darth Vadar, but he was just as evil!

Mr. Durkins turned and peered into Obi's cage. He fixed his eyes on Obi and said, "So who do you think she wrote about?"

"Excuse me?"

"Rachel. Who do you think she wrote about? You know, for her home-work paper. Who do you think she said is her favorite pet?"

Obi, shocked, stared at Mr. Durkins's shadowy, hunched figure. As dark as the bedroom was, Obi was still able to make out the stern, hard look in his beady eyes.
"How did you know Rachel had to write a homework paper about her favorite pet?"

"Nothing happens in this house without me knowing about it, kid! So who do you think she wrote about? Think she wrote about you?"

"Me?" said Obi, trying to sound surprised. She gave a small, modest laugh. "Oh, heaven's no, not me!"

"Yeah, you're right," said Mr. Durkins. "No way would she write about you."

"Wait, what!?" exclaimed Obi, taken aback. "What do you mean no way would she write about me? Rachel most certainly would so write about me! Why wouldn't she?"

"Why *would* she?" said Mr. Durkins. "You're her oldest pet!"

"I'm not *that* old!" protested Obi. "And besides, what does that have to do with anything?"

"Well, you've been around the longest."

"Yes, that's true, but I still don't see why she wouldn't write about me just because I've been her pet the longest!"

"Well, I think it's perfectly obvious," said Mr. Durkins. "She's grown tired of you!"

"She has not!"